MOON CAKE

Joan Aiken was born in Sussex, not far from where she lives now, and grew up with her mother and stepfather, the English writer Martin Armstrong. Her father was the American poet, Conrad Aiken. She began writing at the age of five, and hasn't stopped since; alongside two marriages and two children. Since the early 1960s, over ninety of her books have been published for both children and adults. Joan Aiken's spellbinding power to captivate readers both young and old grows with every story written.

Also by Joan Aiken and published by Hodder:

Fog Hounds, Wind Cat, Sea Mice
A Harp of Fishbones
The Jewel Seed
Midnight is a Place

Other titles by Joan Aiken:

The Winter Sleepwalker
The Wolves of Willoughby Chase
Black Hearts in Battersea
A Handful of Gold
A Bundle of Nerves
The Kingdom Under the Sea
A Necklace of Raindrops
Tale of a One-Way Street
Past Eight O'Clock

MOON CAKE

and

OTHER STORIES

Joan Aiken

Illustrated by Wayne Anderson

a division of Hodder Headline plc

Published in hardback in Great Britain in 1998
by Hodder Children's Books

This paperback edition published in Great Britain in 1998
by Hodder Children's Books

10 9 8 7 6 5 4 3

A Catalogue record for this book is available from the British Library

ISBN 0 340 70926 X

Typeset by Hewer Text Composition Services, Edinburgh
Printed and bound in Great Britain by
Mackays of Chatham plc, Chatham, Kent

Hodder Children's Books
A Division of Hodder Headline
338 Euston Road
London NW1 3BH

CONTENTS

To my grandchildren
Belou and Emil

MOON CAKE

It was a dismal time for Tom when he had to go and spend some months with his grandfather, the old doctor at Ware-on-the-Cliff. Tom had nothing personally against his grandfather, who was a silent old character, rather deaf, but still able to find out what was the matter with his patients and, generally, cure them. No; there were other troubles.

To begin with, Ware-on-the-Cliff was a spooky little place, halfway down the steep hillside, its ancient stone cottages clinging to the cliff face like moss on roof tiles. In between the houses, the road changed to a flight of steps and led on down to the small harbour below.

There was no other exit from the village. Except by sea, of course. Somewhere out beyond the harbour, nearly always hidden in mist, lay an island. Nobody went to it.

The road to Ware-on-the-Cliff passed through Ware-in-the-Woods, an hour's ride across the forest. The forest was huge and dark and full of wild perils, especially the large, ferocious wolves, which could outrun most vehicles. So people travelling to Ware-on-the-Cliff had to keep their car windows shut and doors locked and drive at top speed. Because of this, very few came.

"I can't think why they come at all," muttered Tom.

His grandfather looked at him thoughtfully.

"They come because they have lost hope," he said.

The people in the village kept themselves to themselves. Some had boats and caught fish, some dug in their steeply-tilted gardens. They sat on their stone walls and stared at the misty sea, at the mist which veiled the island.

"Once a month," a man called Grant explained to Tom, "once a month, it's said, on the night when there's no moon, a boat comes over from the island to the jetty, and then rows back to the island again."

"Who's in the boat?" said Tom, not very interested.

He was helping Mr Grant - for want of anything better to do - on a job in his cottage, knocking down the walls between the small, damp rooms.

"Nobody knows. Some say it's the ghosts of sailors who drowned at sea. Or people who drowned in the bay."

With his sledge-hammer Mr Grant struck a terrific blow at the wall separating kitchen from front room. At once, the ceiling began to crack and sag.

"I think," Tom suggested, "that if you take away that wall, the whole house may collapse. I think that wall holds up the roof."

"Can't be helped. I've got to have a bigger room." Grant struck another angry blow.

A large piece of ceiling fell in. Tom and Grant just managed to get out before the roof collapsed.

"I'll have to find another unused house," said Grant, sighing, "and start again. Lucky thing there are so many empty ones."

"Why do you want such a big room?"

"I was in jail twelve years," Grant said, collecting his tools together. He started down the hill towards another deserted cottage. "For a crime I didn't commit. Shut in a cell the length of a bed. No room is ever going to be big enough again."

"I see," said Tom. But he didn't, altogether.

He glanced past Grant down the hill towards his grandfather who always, at this time in the evening, went to stand on the stone jetty for twenty minutes or so, gazing fixedly at the rocky curve of shore that sloped into the sea beyond the harbour wall. Just now the tide was out: green, weed-covered, scaly rocks were all dotted over with white, quarrelling, hungry gulls.

"Why does Grandfather go and stand and stare at the beach like that every single evening?" Tom asked Mrs Quest, who came in every day to do a bit of cleaning and cookery for the Doctor.

"He's looking at a ghost," Mrs Quest said, taking a pie out of the oven.

"What ghost?"

"The ghost of a young lady on a horse."

"How do you know that?"

"Bless you, he's been doing it every day these last forty years. Everybody knows that," said Mrs Quest, starting to mash a dish of parsnips. "She comes a-riding along the beach, round from the north headland, a-singing to herself, and then she stops on the shore a while, and then she swims her pony out to sea."

"Why? Doesn't she ever come back?"

Mrs Quest shook her head.

"Was she a real person once?"

"Ah, who's to say? But everybody was real once, I do suppose."

Mrs Quest stepped to the front door and vigorously rang the dinner bell. The old Doctor, down on the quay, heard the summons, and began to limp slowly up the hill.

"Why did you come to live in the village, Mrs Quest?" asked the boy, as they stood watching the old man's slow progress. "You haven't always lived here, have you?"

"No, love. See, my hubby, he turned sour, where we lived before, acos he used to go out treasure-hunting with two mates and a metal-detector, searching for buried gold, and suchlike."

"Did they find any?"

"Not my hubby; but one of his mates did, in a field where they all was. Dug up two whole kilos of gold bars, if you'll believe me, from some old Bronze Age lord's hidey-hole. And some bracelets and brooches. And my husband was so sick disappointed, because the other chap had found it, and not him, that he couldn't stand to live there any more. So we come here."

"The other man might have offered to share," said Tom slowly, frowning.

"No, love. 'Twas how they'd agreed it, before, that whoever found anything, it should be his. My hubby had found a bit of an old sword, once, and he kept that. But it turned all to bile, inside him, after his neighbour found such a lot. So we moved." Mrs Quest sighed.

"I see," said Tom. But he didn't, altogether.

Next day Tom was helping another neighbour, Mr Sharp, dig the tangled roots of weeds from his garden patch.

"You haven't been here very long, then, Mr Sharp," Tom said, looking at the brambly, unkempt garden.

"No, my boy. Just last month, we come here."

"Why did you come?"

"Ah, see, it was a legal business. The chap next door to us, he kept a dog. Bark, bark, that dog did, never left off. Enough to drive you wild, it was. Day after day. Week after week. We mentioned it to him, polite, we complained, we made objections, he never took a blind bit of notice."

"So what did you do?"

"Started keeping pigs in my back garden. Twenty of them, beauties. Gloucester Old Spots. Real fond of 'em, Minnie and I got. But the chap next door, he was riled. Couldn't take a hint, see. Said the pigs brought rats. Said they stunk. Well, I told him, pigs are right decent creatures, clean as you or I, give 'em the chance. But our neighbour, he went to law about it. Brought it in that I had committed a nuisance. Big damages, I had to pay. Had to sell all my pigs."

"Shall you keep pigs here?" asked Tom.

"Too steep," said Mr Sharp, gloomily surveying the slope that ran up behind them. "A pig'd fall off that; he'd roll all the way down to the harbour. Goats, yes; goats you could keep here; not pigs. And I don't fancy goats."

With irritable force, he struck his spade into the soil.

"Grandfather," said Tom that night at supper, "why did you come to live at Ware-on-the-Cliff? It must have been a long time ago."

Tom had found that, if he spoke in one exact tone of voice, not too high, not too low, the Doctor, deaf though he was, could catch what was said.

The old man looked at Tom attentively.

"Why did I come to live here? It was for a selfish reason. I was young then. When we are young our feelings can be so strong that they govern us. We commit shocking follies. You will find that out for yourself soon enough. I was happily married to your grandmother; but I fell in love with a young lady. Just from the way she looked! I hadn't even spoken to her. I knew nothing about her. But I moved heaven and earth, shifted my medical practice, uprooted your grand-mamma (who was shortly expecting twins) in order to come and live here, at Ware-on-the-Cliff."

"What happened?"

"Nothing happened. Everything happened. The twins, Edward and Paul, were born."

"I have an Uncle Paul?" Tom was surprised.

"You did have. He is no longer with us. Or his son Paul."

"My cousin," said Tom, astonished.

"No longer with us," repeated his grandfather. "Your grandmother died, when the boys were fifteen. Your father Edward moved away and became a doctor."

"And the young lady?"

"The young lady (who lived in the next village, Hope Hoe, round the north headland) - one day, who knows why? she rode her horse out to sea and was never seen again."

"But Uncle Paul? And my cousin?"

"They . . . vanished. People do vanish here."

"But," said Tom.

"Yes. But. But every day I see the ghost of that girl, riding her horse out to sea. She is as clear to me as you are now, Tom. Whereas your grandmother - heaven rest her good soul - I never see her at all."

"And my Uncle Paul? And his son Paul?"

"Perhaps they went to the island. Who knows? Only some of your questions can be answered, Tom. Why did I come here? Why do I stay? Will that girl's ghost go on riding after I am gone from here? We shall see."

Tom said, "You know why I was sent to

stay with you, Grandfather?"

"Yes, my boy. I do know."

"Because I burned down our house. And Mum and Dad have to find somewhere else to live."

"Yes, I know that," said the Doctor, sadly.

"It was an accident, Grandfather."

"Yes, my poor boy. I believe that it was. It was just a pity that the house where you were born happened to be so old and beautiful. It was a pity that your mother's family had lived in it for five generations."

Tom jumped up and walked quickly about the room.

"Was that my fault?" he demanded. "I didn't *ask* for all these ancestors with their pictures hanging on the walls like - like bats! I didn't ask for all that weight round my neck. How they had lived, what they did, how they had done it! I didn't want it. I'm sorry I burned the place down, I never meant to do *that* - not at *all.* I was just trying something in my room, trying to see if I could make a bomb—"

"And it appears that you succeeded."

"Of course I'm sorry!" cried Tom. "Of course I'm sorry! I told them that! I'm glad no one was killed. But what can I do now? I can't put things back the way they were—"

Somebody knocked at the door.

"I'll go," said Tom. "If it's a patient, what shall I say?"

"That I'll see them in the surgery."

But it was not a patient.

Outside the door stood a skinny woman, dressed in rusty black. Her hair was rusty too, and hung in elflocks round her bold, bony face. Her eyes were green.

"Hello, dearie," she said. "You don't know me, but I know who you are. I'm Mrs Lee, Mrs Lallyday Lee, from the top of the village. The house on wheels."

"Oh, yes I know," said Tom eagerly. "I've often wondered who lives in that house, and how it got there."

"And who painted the pictures too, I'll be bound!"

The wheel-house was covered in wild pictures, painted in brilliant colours, dark-blues and red and gold.

"Do you want to see Grandfather?" said Tom.

"No, it's you I want to see, dear."

"Oh," said Tom, surprised, and he added, "I'd better tell Grandfather." And he put his head round the kitchen door and said, "It's Mrs Lallyday Lee, Grandfather. She says she wants to see me."

Grandfather's spoon, full of damson pudding, halted halfway to his mouth. After a very long silence he said, "Of course she was bound to come sometime. And you were bound to see her. Very well. There is nothing I can say, at the moment."

Puzzled, Tom went back to the front door, where Mrs Lallyday Lee still stood at her ease on the step, as if she had stood on many steps in her life.

"All right, dear?" she said, smiling. "I was sure your granda wouldn't raise any objections. Well, now I'll tell you. This is the plan. I'm making a Moon Cake."

"A Moon Cake, Mrs Lee? What's that?"

"A Moon Cake, dearie, can only be made in a very special way, and by special folk . . . I'm one as can make them. You need a passel of things for it - peaches, and brandy, and cream. And some powdered sea-horse. And a handful of green-glass tree snails. And the cake has to be made when the moon's growing up to its full size. And the cake has to be mixed by the light of the moon's beams. And then," said Mrs Lee impressively, "the cake has to be eaten on a night when the moon's gone altogether."

"Same as the boat to the island," Tom said, remembering.

"What's that, dear? Oh. Yes. But that's *nothing* to do with my cake." Mrs Lallyday Lee frowned, seeming a little put out.

"But what's your cake *for*, Mrs Lee? Why all the rules? I don't understand."

"What's my cake *for*? Why, Master Curiosity, my cake (and there's only one of its kind mixed and munched in a generation), my cake is certainly not for every Tom, Dick, and Harry - though, to be sure, we'll hope there's a young Tom going to get a nibble of it this time round," Mrs Lee said, showing a great many brilliant white teeth in her brown face as she smiled. "What's my cake for? Why, it's to put the clock back, that's what it's for, to be sure!"

"What does that mean, Mrs Lee? I still don't understand."

Mrs Quest bustled by, on her way home to her own cottage. Much to Tom's surprise, her usually friendly face seemed extremely *un*friendly, and she hurried past in silence, twitching her skirts aside from Mrs Lee.

"How often have I heard somebody say," Mrs Lee went on, eyeing Tom narrowly, "how many times have I heard some poor soul cry out, 'Oh, if only I could put things back the way they were!'"

"The way they were," repeated Tom slowly.

"The way they were before something bad happened. Before somebody got sent to jail, or his friend dug up the gold, or before a man fell out with his next-door neighbour, or fell in love with the wrong person. Or before the child died! That's often a grievous landmark with young parents. I've known a-many and a-many . . . Or before the house burned down."

"Before the house burned down."

"See? Now you're catching on! Now you are getting the idea. So: all you have to do is help me make the Moon Cake. A person your age has to help."

"Help you? How can I do that?"

"I need three friends to help. That's always the way it is. One to bring the brandy, and one to bring the sea-horses. Those are little shells, you know. They have to be powdered up. And one must bring the green-glass tree snails. And that's the job for you, Tom, my boy."

"Green-glass tree snails?" Tom had never heard of such things. "Where in the world would I find those, Mrs Lee?"

"Oh, dearie, you can easily find them under the beech trees that grow up at the top of the cliff."

"Isn't it a bit dangerous up there?" The forest, full of wolves, Tom understood, ran up from far inland to the very lip of the cliff.

"Oh, surely not for you, my dearie. Why, every wolf in the forest knows and respects your granda."

Tom doubted this. But he hated to seem a coward.

"What do they look like, Mrs Lee? The snails?"

"Tiny little green shining things. Just like their name. Green-glass shells, they have. Not much bigger than seed pearls, they are, and the shells are like water, like glass, you can see right through 'em."

"How many do you need?"

"A dozen, my boy. Say thirteen, just for luck! You'll find them around the roots of the beeches, or on the trunks. You're best to look for them on a bright sunny day, otherwise you won't catch the shimmer of their tiny shells. Once you've spotted the first, then you'll notice a-many more. And then you bring 'em to me and then I'll make the Moon Cake. And then us'll see what us'll see."

Her eyes gleamed oddly. Tom said, "Have you made many Moon Cakes, Mrs Lee?"

"Haven't had the chance, my boy, but my grandma taught me how. To help all those that wishes to go backwards to where they were before."

"But what about those that don't?"

"Ah, they can please theirselves, can't they? But us don't care about *them*! Just you get me those snails, my boy. Take a jam-jar, or an old cocoa-tin, so they doesn't turn all to dust in your breeches pocket. And then you fetch them up to my house and I'll show 'ee the pictures, inside as well as outside."

She walked away up the hill, and Tom turned indoors to his unfinished supper.

"Well," said the Doctor, giving his grandson a penetrating glance under his bristly brows, "and what did Mrs Lee want?"

"She wants to make a Moon Cake."

"A Moon Cake," repeated the Doctor in tones of considerable disgust. "And of course she needs a young person to help her. You."

"Yes," said Tom, and then he asked in a hesitating voice, "do you forbid it, Grandfather?"

"I? Forbid? What right have I to do that? No, my boy, you must take your own path. But don't imagine the woman is doing it for *your* benefit. No, she has her own reasons. Who else is helping her? Mr Grant? Mr Sharp?"

"I don't know, Grandfather."

"Not Mrs Quest?"

"I don't think so," Tom said, remembering Mrs Quest's look of dislike as she passed by.

"I hope not." And the Doctor added, as if it were relevant, "Mrs Quest's husband died last year."

The next day was sunshiny, as much as days ever were at Ware-on-the-Cliff; a mild sun peered doubtfully through the mist. Tom took an old tin box that had once held his grandfather's pipe tobacco and made his way up the hill, past the last houses, and the gardens full of cabbages, and the gorse bushes, to where the forest began. Great beech trees stood like the advance guard of an army; but, due to the west wind which blew so strongly for ten months of the year, they did not stand up straight, but leaned eastwards, so that the crest of them, on top of the hill, slanted like the plume on a Roman soldier's helmet.

Tom went a short way in, among the trees. He did not go far, because of the wolves. Ahead of him the forest was black dark, where the trunks clustered closer together and the canopy of leaves overhead kept out the daylight. Underfoot the soil was soft and brown and crumbly, from years of rotting leaves.

For ever, thought Tom, walking very quietly between trees. I suppose this forest has been here *for ever.* You couldn't put this forest back the way it was, because it always was.

And then he remembered his dream.

He remembered his dream because his tongue was still painfully sore. When Tom's dreams became too frightening, he bit his tongue, and woke himself out of them. Last night's dream had been one of that kind. It had taken place in a forest, but the forest was full of water. Sharks had been swimming among the trees, huge deadly sharks with black backs and white, smooth, terrifyingly under-hung jaws, full of brilliant razor-sharp teeth.

Tom paused, remembering the awfulness of his dream. He thought: perhaps, once, the sea was all over the top of this cliff, perhaps where I am now was deep under water. Was the moon still there, then? Up above?

He looked down at the ground. And he saw an active twist of adders, young adders, a whole family of them, newly hatched, wriggling and squirming, all tangled together, not a shoe's length ahead of his right foot.

He stood stock-still, his breath suspended, his skin icy with fright. Tom really hated snakes. And these were deadly ones, he knew. Not one bite, perhaps, but half-a-dozen - as there must be here - half-a-dozen snake bites could easily finish you off. Very cautiously, he took himself backwards, making a close study of every patch of ground where he intended to set a foot. And so he suddenly began to notice the green-glass tree snails, shining here and there in the beech mast like tiny twinkling emerald beads. Some were on the beech roots, some on the trunks of the trees.

Tom saw more adders, as well. One lay curled up, very peacefully, fast asleep, in a tidy symmetrical flat coil, with its head in the middle. One was making its purposeful way among the beech crumble, minding its own business. One wary, uncertain, weaving its head to and fro; Tom moved well away from that one, and went in a different direction. It resembled somebody, he couldn't think who. He saw no wolves.

By now he had collected enough green-glass tree snails, surely, for anybody's need; so he turned, with great relief, out of the beechwood into the daylight, and made his way down, right down through the village, until he came to the stone jetty where the old Doctor was keeping his evening vigil.

Tom, following the old man's intent stare, could see nothing at all on the beach; but he asked, "Is she there, Grandpa? The young lady?" and the old man, without moving his head, answered, "Yes, she's there."

Twenty minutes went by, and Mrs Quest rang the dinner bell from above; grand father and grandson walked slowly up the hill. The Doctor asked, "Did you get the tree snails, my boy?" and Tom said, "Yes, here they are, Grandfather, aren't they beautiful?"

"Too beautiful to be put into the Moon Cake, don't you think?" said the old man, looking at the contents of the tin. "Or, at least, not the live ones."

"I hadn't thought of that," said Tom.

Because the shells were transparent, it was easy enough to sort out the ones which still had live snails inside. In the dusk, after supper, Tom ran up the hill to the edge of the forest and returned the live snails to their proper home. There were still plenty left. Then he went downhill again to where the house on wheels stood, sideways to the slope, among brambles and gooseberry bushes in a patch of deserted garden.

"I've brought you the snail shells, Mrs Lee!" Tom called.

Her head emerged through the open door at the end of the wagon, and she came smiling down the three steps.

"Ah! that's my boy! Let's see, then."

She studied the collection in the tobacco tin. "'Tis a grand lot you brought; only a great pity there's no live snails among 'em. They make the cake fresher, so."

"Oh," said Tom.

"And Mr Grant's brought me the sea-horses and now I'm only waiting for the peaches and brandy from Mr Sharp . . . tonight's the last night before the full moon, so 'tis a fine timely night for mixing the cake."

"What do you mix it in, Mrs Lee?"

"Anything that's about!" cried she, laughing gaily. "From a copper's riot-shield to a baby's bath. But the spoon that mixes it must be made of hazel-wood, no other; and the moon's rays must be mixed in, ninety-nine times, neither more nor less; so no person can help me with the stirring, but only myself, lest I be distracted and lose count."

Tom thought that would be very easy.

Where does she do the mixing? he wondered, but thought it best not to ask.

She caught hold of the question in his mind, though, and said, "You wish to know where I do the mixing. But I'll not be telling you, for fear you might come to peep and distract me. Best you should not know. I'll show you the bowl, though, that will hold the mixture. Come into the house, boy."

Tom followed her into the van, the inside of which was painted as brilliantly as the outside. But it was smothered in dust and cluttered with largish things: a loom, a spinning-wheel, a copper cauldron, a baby's cradle, tools, lamps, old clothes, kitchenware, all higgledy-piggledy. Mr Grant wouldn't like it here, thought Tom, he'd never put up with living in such a small place, so untidy, and all covered in dust, too. It must be a long time since any baby slept in that cradle . . .

And again, as if she had caught his thought, Mrs Lee said, "Yes, I did have a baby, long ago, who slept in that cradle . . . But when he learned to walk he wandered off, perhaps into the sea; he never came back."

For a moment she had stopped smiling. But then she nodded in a spritely manner and said, "Tomorrow night the cake shall be mixed. And taken next day to Mr Pentecost the baker. For I've no oven big enough to hold it. Mr Pentecost will bake the cake as it should be cooked, slow and easy. Then it must rest for ten days, and on the tenth, each of you helpers shall have a slice. This-here's the mixing-bowl, see: a baby's bath."

It was an old one, made of papier-maché, faded blue. Just for a moment Tom thought he saw a little ghost in it, looking at Mrs Lee.

Nervous, uneasy, though she invited him to stay, he took his leave and ran back to his grandfather's house.

Next day was close and thundery. Tom kept thinking about the cake, slowly baking in Mr Pentecost's oven. Mr Pentecost was the oldest man in the village. He had been born at Ware and had seen children and grandchildren come and go. Sometimes he walked up the hill and played a game of chess with the Doctor. His oven was huge, set into a wall. He would take and bake in it anything that people brought him: pasties, loaves of bread, pies, birthday cakes. He made no comment on the food that customers wished to bring to him, just slid the pans in on his great flat spade, and later on slid them out again. "My oven's a hundred years old," he sometimes said, "and it will still be here in a hundred years' time. Baking's one thing folk will never do without."

A smell of hot bread generally hung about the village, competing with the salt, briny, seaweedy smell of the harbour.

But while Mrs Lee's cake was in the oven a different scent intruded: a close, heady, musty scent like that of wine or beer brewing. Tom didn't care for it.

Dark had fallen by the time the cake was

done, and Mrs Lee carried it slowly back to her house, covered with a cloth.

"No, no, you can't see it!" she said to Tom, passing him in the street. "Not yet! It has to rest, now, for ten days."

"As if it were alive," thought Tom. "Could a cake be alive? A cake in the shape of a small person? Could it think?"

A crack of thunder sounded overhead.

"Be a storm, one of these days, most likely," said old Mr Pentecost, cleaning out his oven with a long-handled brush and pan. "Now, Tom, lad, you take these sweepings and toss them down the cliff. I reckon the gulls are welcome to them."

Tom took the panful of burnt, dark-smelling crumbs and tossed them over the cliff wall, down on to the beach. But the gulls ignored them.

"Tide will soon wash them away, though," said Mr Pentecost when Tom told him this. "A good clean tide will wash away anything."

"Don't you like Mrs Lee's Moon Cake?" Tom asked.

Mr Pentecost gave Tom a long look, under his white brows.

"Trade's trade," he said at last. "I bake whatsoever I'm given. But no, I don't. That ain't a right mix. Sooner that cake's out o' the village, the better I'll be pleased. That cake's a-lying up there, in her place, like a magnet, like a target. Pulling down trouble. Put that cake in a boat, the sharks'd follow it, like they follow the scent of blood."

"*Sharks,* Mr Pentecost?"

"Manner o'speaking, boy. There's a-many harmful things beside sharks. Run you home, now, get you to your rest, tell your granda I'll be along, presently, for a game to settle our spirits."

Tom ran back to his grandfather's house. That night the storm never really broke, but rumbled and sputtered, with faint hiccups of thunder and twitches of sheet lightning. And, over the next ten days a hot, dull, thunderous air hung over the village; and the doughy, resinous odour of the cake never seemed to leave its narrow lanes. As the moon dwindled, the smell grew stronger. Tom had always been fond of the moon, but now it seemed to him like something that had gone mouldy and was rotting away in a corner of the sky.

On the tenth afternoon Mrs Lee met Tom in the street.

"'Tis tonight, then, our picnic, eh, Tom, boy?" she said, showing all her teeth in a wide grin. "You and me and t'other two fellows, down on the strand, us'll have a fine randy, won't us? You come a-nipping down the steps, half after eleven, so's to be ready on the shore. And then us'll see what us'll see!" Her eyes sparkled.

But Tom said, "I'm not coming to your picnic, Mrs Lee."

Her face changed completely. Cold eyes, like a snake's, stared at him. She said, "Your granda won't allow you? Eh? Is that it?"

"No," said Tom. "But I've changed my mind. What's done is done. Things have got to keep going on. Otherwise it's just like playing a game. And it's not a game."

"You'll be sorry," Mrs Lee spat at him. "Oh, you'll be *very* sorry, Mister Clever Tom!

All alone on the hillside while others gets their heart's desire! And *he'll* be sorry too!" she hissed after him. "So proud as he is! So puffed up. His'll be the loss!"

"Yes," said Tom. "Well. Goodbye, Mrs Lee."

He walked on up to his grandfather's house, where the two old men were playing their game of chess.

"I'm going to bed," said Tom. The Doctor's bristly brows shot up.

"Decided to forgo your slice of cake, have you?" he said. "Wise boy! There's better things round the corner." And he called something which Tom didn't catch as he went upstairs, perhaps about slips between cups and lips?

Tom climbed into bed and fell asleep at once, and dreamed of nothing. But then later he woke up, crossed his bedroom floor to kneel with elbows on the low stone sill, and looked down through the window at the strand far below. The moon was gone, the night was dark. He could see the faint prickle of a bonfire, down on the shore. And then he thought he saw a small, pale light come bobbing over the waves towards the beach. Could it be a boat, making for the light of the fire?

Next moment the close calm of the night was splintered by a single earth-shaking crash of thunder, and a blue-white dagger of lightning drove straight from the top of the sky to the place on the shore where the fire had burned. No other sound followed. The village seemed to hold its breath.

After a while Tom heard the startled cries of sea-birds and flapping of wings. And the wash of large waves.

He went downstairs to the two old men.

"Never expected owt else," Mr Pentecost was saying. "Did you, then? Asking for trouble, that were. Making that cake."

"Should we go down to the shore?" said Tom, trembling. "To - to see if there's anything we can do?"

"Past helping, I reckon," said Mr Pentecost.

"Or don't need *our* help, at all events,"

said the Doctor. "Morning will be time enough to go down there."

In the morning they found a large burnt patch on the rocks; but the tide had come in and out since last night's thunder-clap. Anything that might have been left on the shore was washed away.

"Best as things are," said the Doctor.

Mrs Lee, Mr Grant and Mr Sharp were absent from their homes.

At dusk Tom, from a perch on the cliff, unseen by his grandfather, watched in queer disquiet as the old man made his usual pilgrimage down to the jetty. And Tom went on watching as the Doctor peered and stared, and shook his head, and peered again, and, at last, giving up, made his slow way back home.

"Couldn't you see her, Grandpa?" Tom asked unhappily, meeting the old man at the door.

"No, my boy."

"But, Grandpa - *she was there*! *I* saw her - the young lady - riding her grey pony. Over the burnt rocks. I saw her. She was there."

"Not for my eyes, any more," said the old man. "To be sure, it's time I forgot her. But see - here's a letter from your father." Opening it, he read, "We have found a new house, and shall be ready to have Tom back with us as soon as he is ready to come."

"Oh, Grandfather!"

"Yes; it's time you left Ware, my boy. Back to begin where you left off. But maybe, one day, you'll come back. And, if you do," said the Doctor, "who knows? Perhaps the young lady will be waiting for you."

BARMKINS ARE BEST

Once there was a girl called Anna Freeway. She was not very big. Her father, Mr Freeway, was the owner of a huge chain of supermarkets. They were called Freeway Stores. Mr Freeway was very, very busy all week, running his stores. He worked in an office sixty storeys up. From its window you could see the sea, far away. But Mr Freeway never had time to look out of the window and see the sea.

Every Sunday, Mr Freeway took Anna for a walk. They always went Anna's favourite way - past the vet's surgery, where there were two big stone lions on each side of the door, past the war memorial where there was a big wreath of flowers, past the pond where there were swans and ducks, on to the common where there were gulls, and boys flying kites.

Mr Freeway never talked much. But Anna didn't mind. She liked looking about - at two pennies somebody had dropped on the path, at a sparrow that flew past carrying a bus ticket in its beak, at a man wheeling his rubber boots on a trolley. And she wondered about these things. Was the sparrow going to catch a bus, or had it just got off one? Who had dropped the pennies? Were the man's boots so tired that they had to be wheeled?

One day Mr Freeway was even quieter than usual. He was worried. By and by Anna noticed that he hadn't said anything for half an hour.

She said, "Why are you so quiet, Pappy?"

He said, "I'm worrying."

"Why are you worrying?"

"Because I'm trying to think of a way to make people buy more food from my stores. And I can't."

"Why should people buy more food?"

"So they can eat more."

"Don't they eat enough as it is?" said Anna. She looked round. She could see quite a few fat people.

"Not all of them," said Mr Freeway. He looked round, too, and saw quite a lot of thin people.

"What happens if they buy more food?"

"We get richer."

"But aren't we quite rich already?"

"You could have a TV set in your bedroom," said Mr Freeway.

Anna thought about that. She liked to sit watching TV in the main room, leaning against her mother, while Joe played tigers. Joe was her brother. He would have liked to come out with them. But Mr Freeway said that he was too much of a handful.

"I don't think I want a TV in my bedroom," Anna said finally.

"Well, we could have three cars."

"Who would drive the third car?"

"It could be there in case something went wrong with the others."

Anna thought about this for a long time. Then she began thinking about other things. How do squirrels *know*, when they jump from one branch to another, that the second branch won't break? What happened to knights wearing armour when they wanted to go to the bathroom? Suppose your arms started to argue with your legs, which would win? Suppose your legs said they wouldn't walk any more? Suppose your hands wouldn't pick things up unless you gave them a treat?

What *would* be a treat for your hands?

Anna and her father walked for a long way in silence.

At last he said, "What are you thinking about, Anna?"

She said, "I'm thinking about barmkins."

"And what are barmkins, may I ask?"

Anna thought hard for a long time. Then she said, "Barmkins are things that I think about when I'm not thinking about anything else."

"What do they look like?"

"There are lots of different kinds. They can look like almost anything."

Anna looked round her - at the grassy

common, the blue sky, the bare trees, the white houses in the distance, a helicopter up above, the red buses going along Park Side Road, at the running dogs, and the flying kites.

Her father said, "Are barmkins good or bad?"

Anna thought about that for a long time too.

Then she said, "It depends where they are. A stone is good on the path, but bad in your shoe. An ice cream is good in your hand, but bad down your back." Looking at a tree upside down in a puddle, she said, "A tree is good out of doors but bad when it grows up through your bath." She thought some more and said, "Joe is bad when he's awake, but good when he's asleep."

Joe, Anna's younger brother, was clever, strong, and beautiful, but wild. While Anna and her father walked on the common, he was at home, hindering their mother from making lunch.

Anna's father said, "So where would barmkins be bad?"

Anna thought, and said, "Well they might be bad in a bowl of jelly, for instance."

Mr Freeway said, "Anna, I think you have given me a very good idea."

They walked home in silence. Mr Freeway was thinking about barmkins.

Outside the vet's surgery, Anna stopped to give each stone lion a kiss.

Next day in his office, sixty floors up, Mr Freeway called all the heads of all his stores together. There were fifty of them, so it was lucky that it was a huge office.

Mr Freeway said, "Ladies and gentlemen, I have thought of a very good way to tempt people to buy more Freeway Foods. We have already told the public that our foods are the freshest, purest, finest, tastiest, cheapest, and healthiest foods they can find anywhere in the world. Our bread is the best, our soups and sausages are the most savoury, our cakes the creamiest, our fruit the finest, our buns the biggest, our muffins the munchiest."

"Yes," everybody said.

"But, just the same, other supermarkets

are now beginning to sell just as much food as we do. So now *we* have to sell *more*!"

"Yes," they all said again.

"And I have thought of a way to do this. We shall tell our customers that all of our foods - the flour, the eggs, the milk, the fruits and vegetables, the sauces, pickles and relishes, the jams, marmalades and spreads, the cakes and biscuits, and the coffee and tea and fizzy drinks, are *absolutely and entirely free from barmkins.*"

"What are barmkins?" somebody asked.

"Nobody knows! That's the great thing. But they might be very bad. Who can tell? They almost certainly *are* bad. And certainly they are not the kind of thing you want to find in your biscuits or your bottles of soda. Barmkins are bad for you. That is what we have to tell our customers. And there are no barmkins, no barmkins whatsoever, in any Freeway Foods."

Mr Freeway's staff thought this a very good plan. So huge posters were printed, and new labels for cans of soup and packets of flour, and for chocolate bars and frozen-food boxes and juice bottles:

THIS FOOD PRODUCT CONTAINS ABSOLUTELY NO BARMKINS.

Then there were advertisements shown on television:

"Nobody wants barmkins in the corners of his refrigerator. You don't want barmkins in the larder, or the store cupboard. Barmkins may lurk unseen where you least expect them. Barmkins may breed at the rate of thousands every day. What can you do to keep barmkins at bay? Unseen barmkins can damage your teeth - give you heartburn - upset the baby - spoil picnic fun. Don't give barmkins a chance! Always shop at Freeway Stores."

For a long time, Mr Freeway's plan was a huge success.

More and more people bought food from his stores.

More and more people began to believe in barmkins. They wrote articles about barmkins in newspapers and magazines, saying that barmkins were a health hazard, that they slowed down the heartbeat and the rate of children's growth. Doctors said that barmkins might give you sore gums, or make your hair fall out. People began to say that they had *seen* barmkins.

Other stores soon began to copy Mr Freeway's idea.

They, too, said there were no barmkins in their frozen chickens or their instant soups.

Mr Freeway was very annoyed at this.

"I had the idea for barmkins first," he said, forgetting that it had really been his daughter Anna's idea.

But there was nothing he could do about it.

For, quite soon, barmkins were everywhere - slogans on T-shirts and the sides of taxis and tube-trains said: *Watch out for barmkins! Gare aux barmkins! Achtung - barmkinnen! Beware of barmkins! Barmkins bite!*

By now, Mr Freeway was very rich indeed. He had four cars, seven telephones, and a TV set in every room. There was even a TV set in the bathroom, and little Joe caught a terrible cold, lying in the bath one evening until the water was icy, watching a programme called *Barmkin Blast-Off*, all about barmkins in outer space.

Little Joe's cold started with shivering and snuffling. Then he began to cough. Then he refused to eat his tea or his supper or his breakfast. Then he was found to have a fever and a headache, and had to be put to bed. Then he became VERY ILL INDEED. Nobody but the doctor and Mrs Freeway might go into his room.

Mr Freeway and Anna were dreadfully miserable and sat about the house doing nothing.

"Oh why, why didn't I take him for walks?" said Mr Freeway.

"You said he was too much of a nuisance," said Anna.

"When he is better I will buy him a TV set to hang over his bed."

"He would rather come for walks with us," said Anna. "And talk to us."

"What about?"

"Grown-up things," said Anna.

"Whatever *we* talk about. Barmkins."

Just now, barmkins were dreadfully on little Joe's mind. He said he could see them in every corner, and that they were coming to get him. He woke screaming from terrible nightmares.

One night Anna heard him.

She jumped out of bed and tiptoed to Joe's room. Mrs Freeway had gone down to the kitchen to warm up some milk, leaving the door open. Little Joe was huddled in one corner of his bed, with his hair standing straight up on end.

"There's two barmkins over there, hiding in the closet!" he told Anna.

She climbed on to the bed and held him tight.

"But, Joe," she said, "barmkins are *good.* Barmkins *love* you!"

"Yes! To eat me all up!" said Joe, trembling.

"No - they won't! Barmkins are really, *really* nice! They are gentle and friendly. They like to sing songs. Shall I sing you a barmkin song, Joe?"

"Yes," he said, rather doubtfully.

But Anna, holding him tighter still, sang,

"Beautiful barmkins, bright and busy
Bubbly barmkins, frothy and fizzy,
Cast your spell - make Joe well -
Now he's not sick any longer - is he?"

Just then, Mrs Freeway came into the room, carrying a mug of hot milk.

"Oh, my gracious goodness, Anna," she said, "whatever are you doing in here? You should be in your own bed."

Mr Freeway was behind his wife, looking pale and worried.

"Joe was frightened of barmkins," said Anna. "But he isn't any more, are you, Joe? Look!" and she skipped across the room and opened the cupboard. "See, there's two barmkins in here, but they are *good* barmkins. And they *love* you, Joe. In fact, they'd like to come and sit on your bed and have you stroke them while you drink your milk."

"All right," said Joe, after thinking carefully about it. "But tell them they must keep very quiet so as not to spill the milk."

He drank the milk, and the barmkins kept quiet. Then he lay down and went to sleep. Mr and Mrs Freeway and Anna tiptoed away to their beds.

And, next morning, Joe was better.

"Pappa," said Anna, "you have got to tell everybody that barmkins are *good*."

"But then," he said sadly, "nobody will want to buy Freeway Foods any more than any other kinds."

"Does that matter?" said Anna. "People are sure to buy *some* of yours. People buy an awful lot of food."

"Well," he said, "I'll have to see."

But already - somehow - the news had leaked out. Articles began to appear in medical magazines:

BARMKINS ARE NECESSARY TO HEALTH.

It has been proved that a lack of barmkins in the diet may create severe problems.

Barmkins are beautiful!

All the food stores began sticking labels on their cakes and candies, their chops and chickens and chutneys, their milk and margarine and melons, saying, "Our products are full of healthy, natural barmkins! Nothing has been removed! No barmkins have been taken away. Taste the fresh real flavour. Barmkins are the best!"

And little Joe went for a walk on the common every Sunday with his father and big sister. He was a terrible nuisance: he chased dogs, and ran into the road, and picked up things he shouldn't, and wanted ice cream all the time, and refused to come away from the slide, and hit other boys.

"But I expect he'll get older by and by," Anna said.

And all the time they talked - about horses and helicopters and squirrels and submarines and Mount Everest and the moon and cheese and computers and sardines and Santa Claus.

And about barmkins.

THE FEATHER AND THE PAGE

The doctor told us that she couldn't last more than a few hours.

"Going very peacefully, your mum," he assured us. "Pity your dad couldn't be here."

Dad, a merchant seaman, was in the Pacific, out of reach.

My sister Hannah sent me off to afternoon school.

Tall and bossy is Hannah, ten years older than me. Blue eyes and fair hair, like Dad. I expect that's why she's always been Mum's favourite.

"No sense in having you hanging round all afternoon, getting under foot, Tim," she said. "Crying and carrying on and asking questions, upsetting Mum when she ought to be quiet and settled. If you gotta cry and ask questions, better do it at school."

So she shooed me off with a push and a shove.

"Can't I say goodbye to Mum?"

"Call goodbye through the window, that way it won't be troublesome to her," says Hannah. Mum was in bed in the downstairs front, easier for doctors' visits and carrying trays.

So I called goodbye, but I don't know if Mum heard me. Anyway she never answered.

I heard Hannah's feet running fast upstairs.

Of course I knew what she was getting. Some of her poems to read aloud to Mum.

You'd never think she'd write poems, my sister Hannah, to look at her, so tall and bustling and bossy as she is. But she'd written quite a stack of them, and even had one or two published in *The Avon Argus*. And what she likes to do, best of all, is read 'em aloud to Mum as she's working on them - used to, that is - and Mum would listen and comment, sometimes make suggestions, alter words.

Again and again I've heard them doing that, while I sat in the back kitchen trying to get on with school work.

Well - I didn't do much work at school *that* afternoon. As you might guess. In fact Miss Lewis, feeling sorry, sent me home early.

Early as Miss Lewis sent me, it was too late for Mum. She'd gone. And she was already laid out, neat and pale, on the bed in the downstairs front, with neighbours coming in and paying respects. Bringing flowers and bowls of custard and quiches.

I felt bad, as you can suppose. Because I'd had no chance to be there when she went, to say a proper goodbye. My own goodbye.

"Did something *come* for her?" I asked Hannah. "Was there a wind? A light? A big clap of thunder? What did Mum say? What happened?"

"Oh, be quiet, you little clunch," Hannah shouted. "It's not like that at all. She just went quietly. In fact—"

In fact, Hannah was too angry to tell me, but I found out later, by listening to what she told Mrs Wickens, that Hannah herself hadn't even noticed when Mum slipped away. She'd been reading one of her poems out loud, and Mum had been repeating bits of words here and there, drowsy but following; and then - I suppose - there came a sort of a gap, and when Hannah next looked up from the page, Mum had quietly left the room. All the listening part of her, that is.

No wonder Hannah was upset about it.

I felt sorry for her, but I couldn't help wondering if Mum had mentioned *me*, at all, in there; whether she might have said, "Will you say goodbye to Tim," or, "Tell Tim to be a good boy, work hard at school and not forget to brush his teeth." Something like that. But, if she did, Hannah never said. And I felt so sad and sick and hollowed-out, at that time, that I never liked to ask.

When somebody has left, and you never had a chance to say a proper goodbye, it leaves a kind of a ragged hole, like a job that's not been decently finished. Days, weeks after, I felt as if I had an injury, raw, hurting, not rightly healed.

What Hannah felt, just then, I don't know; she never talked to me and I never talked to her. Except to say things like, "Have you heard from Dad?" and "Hurry up and make your bed."

Miss Lewis, at school, said, "Tim, you're getting very thin," and, "That sister of yours looks as if she could do with a tonic. When does your dad get back home?"

"Not till after Christmas, Miss."

That was three months off. It had been a long, hot, dry summer, with a huge apple crop. Everybody's trees, all along the village street, were loaded with fruit; you couldn't give apples away. They lay rotting on the grass everywhere. When I lay awake at night, thinking about Mum, wondering where she was now, I'd hear apples falling from the drooping branches: thump, thump; a dull, heavy sound; and then thump, thump, again. In other years Mum used to make pots and pots of apple jelly, slicing and boiling till the juice came a clear, pale red, while Hannah read aloud bits of her poems. But this year Hannah hadn't the heart, she just let the fruit lie.

We had a quince tree, as well, covered with quinces, and Sue Wickens said to me in the school playground one day,

"My mum'd dearly like some of your quinces, Tim Pardon, if as so your sister Hannah don't reckon to use 'em."

"I'll ask her," I said, and Hannah said, "She's welcome. Tell her she can have all she wants. You and Sue can pick them. I can't be bothered."

"Dad'll be sorry, come Christmas," I said. "No quince jelly."

"Oh, what's it to you? Hurry up, you'll be late for school."

So Sue and I picked four baskets of quinces, heavy, hard, yellow, scented things, and took them along to Mrs Wickens.

I was always a bit nervous of Mrs Wickens. She was short and stout, mottled and wrinkled like a lizard. Her eyes were deep, dull-coloured, like holes in her face. Sue's eyes were the same colour, but they shone. In the village they say that Mrs Wickens knows more than most about herbs and cures and tea-leaves and stars. Things like that. But she was pleasant enough.

She looked over the quinces and said, "Thank your sister kindly, Tim Pardon. And I reckon there's something you want to ask me?"

I hadn't known there was, up to then, but of course she was right. I said, "How can you say goodbye to a person, once they are gone?"

"Ah," said Mrs Wickens, not at all surprised, picking up a quince and rubbing the bloom with her thumb. "Well, there's several ways. You could climb up the Driddle, and stay on the top all night."

The Driddle, some say it should properly be called the Druids' Hill, is the big black lump of mountain that rises up steeply behind the church at the end of the village.

"No, I don't want to do that at all," I said quickly. "Not *at all.*"

"Poor-stomached, are ye, Tim Pardon," said Mrs Wickens. "That won't do, not in a business like this. You gotta show a bit of gumption, a bit of pluck, or you'll get yourself nowhere."

"I don't want to do anything Mum wouldn't have liked. She didn't care for those stories about the Driddle."

"Well then," said Mrs Wickens, "you could go to sleep a-laying face downwards on a big looking-glass. Then, when you wake up at midnight, you'll find yourself a-looking down into a face that's not your own."

"I don't think Mum would like that either," I said quickly. "Anyhow we haven't *got* a big mirror, only the little square one that hangs over the kitchen sink."

"In that case," says Mrs Wickens, rather short and snappish, "there's only one way left for ye."

"What's that, missus?"

"You must go to your mum's grave at sunset, and walk round it seven times, just afore the sun sinks out of sight. Then, if you've done it right, she'll speak to you, and you'll hear her say the very last thing that was on her mind afore she took and died. 'Tis a certain way, that one. I've never knowed it to fail."

"I don't know as I'd dare do that," said I, with my teeth a-chattering.

"Ah, don't ye be such a faint-heart, boy! Your mum'd not hold it against ye. And my Sue would go along with you, to keep ye company, wouldn't ye, Sue?"

"Y-y-yes, Ma," said Sue, but she didn't say it real hearty.

I thought and thought about it, and thought and thought. And, on the third day after that, which was a Saturday, Sue and I took ourselves along to the graveyard.

As I said, the church is at the end of the village, and the graveyard, a small one, is cut out of the steep hill, with the church at one side of it, and two huge sycamore trees, like grandfathers, towering up above on the hill-side, the other side of the stone wall. It's a very private place.

My mum's grave was up at the top end. The green turfs had firmed on it, well enough by now, and all the first lot of wreaths and posies had browned and rotted and been thrown away, but others had been brought, small bunches of Michaelmas daisies and bryony berries and purple scabious and late roses; for Mum had plenty of good friends in the village.

"Where is your sister Hannah?" Sue says to me, a bit nervous. "She won't come along and give us what-for?"

"No," I said. "Hannah's indoors, writing. She's stuck on a poem. She won't budge till she's unstuck."

I always knew when Hannah was stuck that way, for she'd have an angry, tied-in look on her face, as if she'd a mouthful of pebbles and didn't know how to spit them out. Ever since Mum went she had been like that.

"She won't come butting in then," said Sue.

She had picked up seven little red crab apples as we walked up the hill past Mrs Jones's pub, *The Welcome*, where a crab tree leans over the wall. The road was covered with little red fruit the size of marbles.

R.I.P.

"Now then, Tim: I'll drop one of these on the grave each time we walk round it, so as to keep count. One!"

Off we went, hand-in-hand, slowly enough over the long grass and rough ground.

It was a queer, misty-hazy afternoon, not cold, not windy; the sun, near setting, looked like a blood-orange in the 'V' of wooded hills at the far end of the valley road.

Like I said, Sue and I went slowly at first, but soon our fright caught up with us, and we fairly scampered round the second, third, fourth, and fifth times; then we slowed up for the sixth circle and - come the seventh - just as the sun dropped from sight, we were crawling on hands and knees.

My head was only a foot from the turf. I heard a mutter down below - like somebody clearing her throat.

"Oh, please!" I gulped out. "No! Please don't, Mum! I'm - I'm sorry to a-bothered you. I've - changed my mind . . ."

But the mutter rose to a throb, like the

rumble of earth and stones land-falling down a hillside.

Sue clapped her hands over her ears. But I lay icy-cold, dumb, pinned, with my elbows on the damp grave and my head turned sideways on, listening above the low hummock of earth.

So I heard my mother's voice, a bit stifled and clogged at first, as it used to be when the illness took her.

What she was saying seemed to be poetry.

"Lost words - lost rhyme
Lost music - lost time
Where are they found?
In no-man's-ground?

After this day
Where do they stay?
In no-man's way?

Lost love - lost light
Melt into night
Where do they rest?
In no-bird's-nest?"

I heard a scuffle. Sue was off, like a rocket, running downhill, with hands still pressed over her ears, as if she'd been ordered off home by an angel with a fiery sword.

"I'll never—" I heard her gasp, "oh, I'll never - I'll never *ever*—"

Then she was gone, past *The Welcome Inn* and the drooping crab tree.

But I went on lying, flat out, still went on lying there, hugging my mother's grave as if it had been a bolster, for an hour or more, until the mist rose, and the barn owl began to hunt in the sycamore tree, and my sister Hannah came angrily looking for me.

"*Tim*! What in mercy's name are you *doing*? How can you be so naughty - thoughtless - troublesome - how *could* you?"

She took hold and shook me; it was the first time she'd touched me since Mum died.

Because I had dared do what I did, I wasn't scared of Hannah any longer. I felt sorry for her, and, on the way home, I told her, listen, Hannah, listen. These were the words that Mum said, and I was able to tell Hannah some of the words. And she listened. And a flood of tears burst out of her.

"That was it!" she said, gasping. "That was the last poem I made up. But I never wrote it down. The way I had it first - it wasn't quite right. And when Mum said it over - when *she* said it—"

Hannah stopped speaking; and I didn't say anything more; and that was how we walked home. But I thought she was not angry with me any more. She held on to my shoulder all the rest of the way down the hill.

One last thing I had not told her. I almost thought - I *almost* thought - that, after the word *nest*, my mum had gone on to say: "Tell Tim I marked a place for him in a book. I marked it with a feather. Tell him goodbye . . ."

Now I have to find the book. And the page, and the feather. That is the next thing I have to do.

There's lots of libraries.

HOT WATER

When Paul's grandmother, old Mrs Munday, died, Paul was sad; but he was pleased to hear that the old lady had left him some things in her will. Paul and his gran had always got on well, though he used to tease her a good deal, hiding her spectacles in the teapot, and so forth.

She had left him five bundles, assorted sizes, and her parrot, Fozz.

"I've always wanted a parrot," said Paul. "And Fozz is only thirty. He'll very likely live another seventy years. I wonder what's in here?"

He undid a small, lumpy package as the red-and-grey Fozz walked up and down his arm.

There was a thick brown-paper wrapping, and inside that was newspaper, and inside that was a plastic bag, and inside that another plastic bag. In *that* was a tea-bag.

"Pour hot water on it!" said Fozz.

"Well, all right," said Paul, and he put the tea-bag into a cup, and poured boiling water on, and made a cup of tea. Then he drank it.

The next parcel he unpacked was big and soft and no shape at all. Paul undid brown paper and sticky tape, and unwrapped newspaper and tissue paper. Inside that was a plastic bag, and inside that another plastic bag. Inside that was a very dirty shirt.

"Pour some hot water on it!" shouted Fozz.

"Well, all right," said Paul. "I couldn't wear it the way it is. What a queer thing for Granny to leave me in her will."

He put a lot of hot water and soap on the shirt, and rubbed and scrubbed it. Then he rinsed it, and it was still dirty. So he put a lot *more* hot water and soap on it and began all over. This time he got the shirt really clean, and hung it on the line to dry. It was a good shirt, red and green.

"Just my size," said Paul. "I'll remember Granny whenever I wear it."

Next, he unwrapped a small packet wrapped in layers and layers and layers of kitchen foil. When he undid the last, there was a packet of instant soup, tomato flavour, Paul's favourite.

"Pour some hot water on it!" shouted Fozz.

"OK," said Paul, and he poured hot water on the powder and made a bowl of tomato soup, and ate it.

Next, there was a packet inside a huge plastic sack. Inside the sack was a bundle of old lace curtains, and when he had unwound them - there were metres and metres - he found a little flat packet labelled Magic Flower.

"Pour hot water on it!" shouted Fozz. That was all that Fozz ever did say.

"Well, I will," said Paul. He put the

Magic Flower in a jam-jar, and poured hot water on it. Slowly, leaf by leaf, petal by petal, the flower uncurled, growing bigger and bigger, until it filled the whole jar, with green leaves and scarlet and white flowers.

"Oh!" said Paul. "That's beautiful!"

The last package had been left in the freezer. It was the biggest of all - big as a chair, but flat.

"What can it be?" said Paul. He undid the sticky tape, and the quilted wrappings, and, inside those, more quilted wrappings, transparent ones, full of little shining bubbles. "What can it possibly be?" said Paul again.

When he took off the last wrapping, there was an Ike. "Oh!" cried Paul, "I've always, always wanted an Ike."

An Ike is a bicycle made of ice. It had ice wheels, which went round, ice handlebars, ice brakes, ice lights, and an ice saddle. It shone like diamonds.

Paul tried riding the Ike, but the saddle was very cold.

"Pour hot water on it!" shouted Fozz.

Hot Water

"All right," said Paul.

So he poured a kettle of hot water over the Ike and it melted right away - the saddle, the wheels, the brakes, the lights, and the handlebars. All that was left was a large puddle.

"*Now* look what you made me do," said Paul to Fozz.

Then he put on his shirt and went to plant some pansies on Granny Munday's grave. Pansies had always been her favourite flower.

"Put some hot water on them!" shouted Fozz.

"No, you silly bird," said Paul. "You put *cold* water on pansies."

And he watered them with cold water, and went off down the road in his red and green shirt, with Fozz sitting on his arm.

THE GREEN ARCHES

There was three things needed before the charm would work. Rather like making a cake, when you want eggs, flour, sugar: it had to be raining, the day had to be Friday, and I had to have had the Dream the night before.

So, on Thursday nights, I would do everything I possibly could to bring on the Dream - look at pictures in picture books of doors, arches, trees, and forests. I'd sit and think and try to remember all the different times I'd had the Dream. Sometimes it worked, sometimes not.

The Dream chooses its own time to visit me. And, when I wake, I don't always remember; but I know when it has touched me, because I feel very calm when I wake, and things work out well for me that day.

I do still have the Dream, which is a comfort.

Oh. There's a fourth thing I forgot to mention, the most important of all. My brother Bran had to be singing his song.

The words of the song go like this:

"When we say goodbye
And wonder why
It has to be
And shall we never see
Each other's face again
What can I say?

I think that love and pain
Will never die
But last for evermore
I think that they
Carry us like the sea
On to a farther shore."

My brother Bran made up the words, and he made up the tune too. It is a very simple tune, there's only seven notes in it, really, and when you hear it the first time you think that you will easily be able to remember it. The seven notes chase each other round and round in what my brother calls a *fugue*. And, while he sings the words to this tune, he will be playing a trickly, wandering jingle on his guitar, so it is like a bridge covered with vines. You can see the shape of the bridge, and you can see the vines as well. But, afterwards, you can never remember it. *Never.*

My brother Bran plays the clarinet, piano, guitar, and mouth-organ. Or he did, before old Mrs Busby next door began to get so angry with us.

I'll come to her in a minute.

First, I'll tell you about what happens when my brother plays and sings his song.

The start of it all was when I was about six. I was sitting under our kitchen table, playing with a conker and a piece of string. And the music suddenly came into Bran's head, and he sang it. As he played and sang, I found that I wasn't under the table, but outside in the street. Standing up.

Castle Street, where we live, winds uphill in a curve. All the houses on our side are shaped like pieces of pie, wider in front than at the back. Between the houses run narrow alleys, closed off from the street by wooden doors. The paths are very narrow, and the doors are always shut. People don't use them much. Some of the doors I've never even seen open. I used to make up tales about what was behind them - mountains, deserts, palaces.

Well. First, like I say, I was listening to Bran's music, then - suddenly - I was outside Mrs Busby's door beside her house. I walked quickly to the door - I could walk - and lifted the latch. The door opened, and I was inside. The narrow mossy path led straight ahead into a wood. And what a wood! The trees, tall as pylons, had branches that curved up and met like the stone arches in the roof of a church; you couldn't tell where one tree ended and the next began.

My brother Bran's tune carried me forward through the glade - easily, quickly - as if

I were a woodpecker, rising and falling. I knew that I was going to the very heart and centre of the wood, and that I would find something marvellous there.

But I didn't get there. The music stopped. And - in the flick of an eyelash - there I was back sitting under the kitchen table with my string and my horse-chestnut.

"Play that again, Bran!" I begged him, and he did. But - as I soon found - it never works more than once on the same day. And it has to be Friday, and it has to be raining, and I have to have had the Dream the night before.

But Mrs Busby, next door, seemed to hate us more and more. She began complaining about Bran's music and saying she couldn't stand all that row. That was after our dad got a job installing alarm systems in people's houses. The first one he installed - to try it out - was in our own house. And Bran came home from school, didn't know the number you have to tap out on the little keyboard, quickly, as soon as you step through the front door. So the alarm went off. I will say that's just about the loudest noise you can think of. You're afraid it's going to lift the teeth right out of your gums. Or the roof off the house. And, while Bran was running round looking for the bit of paper with the numbers written on it, all Mrs Busby's bees, from the hive in her back garden, rose up in a huge black spiral, like a tornado, and left for ever. And they didn't come back.

So you can see why she had bad feelings against us; though it wasn't exactly our fault, and of course Dad apologised, and offered to replace the bees. But she said no to that, she had her own bee supplier. He brings them in a black van at night. Some people say she's a witch. She's certainly very bad-tempered.

I always looked forward to Fridays, when Bran came home for the weekend, for then he'd play his tune and then - sometimes, but not always - I'd float off to the wood. Sometimes it needed the tune and words both, sometimes only the tune.

Every time, I hoped I'd get to the centre of the wood, and, every time, the music stopped just before that happened.

"If only you'd written the tune just a bit *longer*!" I said to Bran. "If only there were nine notes instead of seven!"

But he said tunes make themselves, like plants growing, you have to take them as they come.

Still, I visited that wood so many times in the next year or two that I felt it belonged to me, and I was sure that, somehow, one day, I'd find my way to the middle.

Time went by. I started at school. Dad took me there in his delivery van.

And Mrs Busby got nastier. The second lot of bees weren't, she said, as good as the ones that had gone. And then she said Bran had got to stop playing his music in our house, for her nerves couldn't stand it. So, after that, Bran had to go off to his friend Ostin Morgan's house. The Morgans live outside the town, where there are no neighbours to complain.

"It's a bit hard on Huw," Bran said to our dad. "He misses the music."

Misses! I felt as if someone had sucked away the air I needed for breathing. Before, Bran had played all through the weekend. And Mrs Busby used to rap angrily on the wall.

Dad said, "We have to live with our neighbours. They've got rights too."

So, what Bran started doing, he'd play his harmonica as he rode down the street on his bike. When he got close to our house he'd play the tune of *When We Say Goodbye*, quite loud, so that I could hear it through our front window.

And - sometimes - that was enough to start me off. Like a leaf in a gale, I floated through Mrs Busby's door and off to the wood.

Birds sing in that wood, and bees hum; there are flowers, primroses, growing at the foot of the trees, and the bees float over them. Their hum is like the wind in telegraph wires. Sometimes I wondered if those were the bees that our alarm signal had driven away from Mrs Busby's garden.

(We never use the alarm system; but Dad says he likes the little red and green eyes, winking, so friendly and welcoming, in the corners of rooms.)

But - will you believe it - even Bran, just riding along on his bike in the street, playing his harmonica, even that was enough to put Mrs Busby in a rage.

"She's got acid instead of blood in her veins," said Dad.

"Poor thing. I pity her, really," said Mam.

And one day, as Bran rode past, playing the tune - and I was just beginning to float off, halfway from our kitchen to the wooden door - Mrs Busby opened her upstairs window and chucked a jugful of water all over Bran.

Perhaps she just wanted to give him a wetting. But it turned out more serious. The cold water in his face made him swerve, right into the way of a big truck that was coming down the hill. The truck braked and skidded into Mrs Busby's gate. And all its load - nineteen tonnes of frozen chip potatoes - crashed over the gate into the path beside her house.

And my brother Bran and his bike were somewhere under all that frozen, heavy load.

They got him out, after a while. And he was taken away to hospital and put in intensive care. Unconscious he was, see, and no way could they find to rouse him. All that music trapped inside, and no door by which it could come out.

"I'm afraid I can't hold out much hope,"

the chief doctor told Dad, after three weeks had gone by.

They'd only let me go to see him once. There he lay, flat on a bed, with tubes feeding into him, and tubes leading out; he looked more like an alarm system than a person. Ostin Morgan's sister Angie wheeled me there in my chair - but when she saw Bran she burst out crying - she and Bran had been good friends - and we had to leave again. I wondered if the tune was running round and round inside Bran's head, the notes chasing each other like rain-drops. As we left, I tried to send a message to him: "Bran! Think of the tune. Remember the tune. It might help you." But I got no answer at all.

The truck driver had not been badly hurt, but the company who owned the truck and the nineteen tonnes of frozen chips were very angry with Mrs Busby; and she was just as angry with them. For it seemed that she had been keeping her new lot of bees in their hives just inside the wooden door, on the path at the side of her house, and the frozen load had fallen on them and finished them off. So the truck owners were going to law, and Mrs Busby was going to law.

"*You* are the ones who have really suffered," Mrs Morgan said to my mam. "With your poor boy hanging like that between life and death, and the little fellow already handicapped the way he is. You are the ones who should be going to law."

"What good would law do us?" says Mam. "Law can't make our boys better."

I had a feeling that, if only Bran's tune could be played for him - if only he could hear it - that might undo some knot or latch that would open a way for him to the world again. If only I could remember the tune! I thought. But that tune is like my Dream - every time, it slips away before you can grab it.

Mrs Morgan surprised me, though.

"My husband has a plan," she said.

Mr Morgan is Bran's music teacher.

"He has written down a song that your son wrote," she told Mam. "And it's going to be played on Radio Camelot next Friday.

And Tom's going to get the doctor's permission to take a transistor into the ward and play it, just in case Bran might be able to hear it."

Mam shook her head doubtfully. "*Nothing* reaches him," she said.

I was sitting in my wheelchair in a corner of the kitchen. And I thought two things. One: when they play it on the radio I shall be able to visit my wood again. But only if I have the Dream the night before. Oh, please, please let me have the Dream!

And the other thought: if only I could get to the middle of the wood, perhaps I could find something there, perhaps I could bring something back, that would help Bran, that would set him free. Bring him home.

I asked Mam, I begged and pleaded to be allowed to go to the hospital when Mr Morgan went in with his transistor, to play the tune. But I was not allowed.

"You can listen to it at home, in the kitchen," said Dad. "Angie Morgan is coming in to sit with you."

It rained, that Friday. It *poured.* Bad weather for bees. They stay at home, in their snug hives.

I'd had the Dream the night before, so I was hopeful. As usual, I could not remember what it had been about, but I could feel the afterglow from it.

At three, Angie switched on the transistor.

"Radio Camelot," said the voice. "Here is a pot-pourri from the hills and the valleys. First, a beautiful song written by a teenage boy, sung by the famous tenor Robin Price." Robin Price, I knew, was a friend of Mr Morgan. He sang Bran's song very well and calmly. No sooner had the first three notes floated from the box than I was away, going through Mrs Busby's entrance, along her path, into my wood. Right to the heart of it.

And what did I find there?

I found my brother Bran, under the green arches, filled with peace and light.

"This is the place to be, Huw," he says to me. "This is the best place. No wonder you were always trying to come back. But it's not your turn just yet. Your turn will come though; don't you fret."

Next - to my utter amazement - I saw Mrs Busby. But she was much smaller. She seemed like a child, looking about her as if she'd been struck dumb with wonder. Staring up at the great green arches above, down at the bees floating among the primroses.

"I didn't know," she kept murmuring. "I didn't know it was like this. And - just next door, all the time!"

Then Bran's tune ended and, with a breaking heart, I was snatched away, back to my own life, my own kitchen. Angie was in oceans of tears, with her head on the table, and the phone was ringing.

I wheeled myself over and answered it.

"I'm afraid it's sad news," said my dad's voice. "Bran did hear the tune. He opened his eyes and smiled at us all. And then he took and died."

Well.

I was sad as could be; and yet I could have been sadder, for I was sure, inside me, where Bran had got to, and I couldn't be sorry for that.

It's a comfort to know where he is. Some day I shall join him, and sometimes, when they play his tune on the radio, I have a chance to get a glimpse of him. If I've had the Dream the night before, that is, and it's a rainy Friday.

Here's a queer thing.

After Dad had rung off, Angie and I looked out of the window. And we saw the sky black, as if a dust storm had blown into our town.

But it wasn't a dust storm. It was bees. All Mrs Busby's first lot had come back, to take up residence in their hives again. But it was too late for Mrs Busby. She, it was found, had died of a heart attack, just about the time they were playing Bran's song on the radio.

She'd got no kin, we heard. She was all alone in the world. Poor woman. So Dad took over her bees. They live in our back yard now, furry, friendly things, and the humming they make is like harp music.

I look after them - it's a thing I can do well, in my wheelchair - and I tell them all that happens.

Sometimes I tell them bits of my Dream, if I remember enough.

It's about coming home, you could say.

HATCHING TROUBLE

In Clawness, once, there used to be a dragon. The town is small - houses, church, school, hotel, grocer and fish-and-chip shop. Up above, the dragon used to sparkle like a green-and-gold bracelet, wound around the hilltop, with her head at the top. Her name was Gleer.

She was friendly and loving - as dragons go. She ate only spiteful people, or litter-louts, or the sort who parked for hours on double lines, or dogs who bit children.

"And who minds losing those?" said Mr Mack the mayor to Mr Campbell the dentist. "Think of the tourists she brings."

This was true. People came from far to see her. They left their cars in the car park by the beach, walked up the hill, paid fifty pence to go through the turnstile, and another fifty pence to feed the dragon. Empty bottles, her favourite food, were kept in a huge bin beyond the gate.

Gleer liked green bottles best (mineral water or wine) then brown (beer or whisky) then plain (tonic, lemonade, or milk).

The trick was to throw your bottle high into the air. When you did this, Gleer unwound her top coil of neck, and snapped the bottle in mid-air with a sudden flashing swoop.

All through the summer, happy visitors kept tossing bottles. Gleer never grew tired of catching them; and the tourists never tired of watching her.

She would also munch up rusty prams, broken TV sets, out-of-order toasters, and dead refrigerators.

But one autumn day, when rain blew coldly off the sea, and there were no tourists because of the dismal weather, a knight came riding into Clawness. He wrote his name - Sir Grandley Upshott - in the guest book of the *Green Dragon* hotel.

"I've come to kill your dragon," he said to Mrs Mack, at the desk.

"Och, maircy on us! Ye must not do that!" she said, very shocked.

"Knights always kill dragons," said Sir Grandley Upshott. "Why else should I come all this way, in such wretched weather?"

When he had washed, and put on a bullet-proof vest, and drunk a cup of tea, he took an umbrella, and a shield, and his electric sword, and walked up the hill.

He was indignant at being asked to pay at the turnstile.

"Fine thing - when I'm here to rid you of a pest!"

"Pest?" said Mrs Campbell, who took the gate-money. "Our fine dragon's no pest. She eats more rubbish than any other in the kingdom."

"Dragons are vermin," said Sir Grandley. He walked on up the hill and gave the nearest bit of the dragon - her hind leg - a poke with his sword.

Very startled indeed - for no one had

poked her in a hundred years - Gleer unwound a coil of her gold and scaly neck. Sir Grandley threw up a whisky bottle, which he had taken (without paying) from the bin. Gleer shot out her long fiery tongue and snapped it in mid-air. But that was her last snap, for Sir Grandley whipped out his electric sword and cut off her head.

"Save us!" cried Mrs Campbell. "What in the world did you want to go and do that for?"

"To rid you of a peril," said Sir Grandley, and he put the dragon's head in a large plastic bin-bag which he had carried, folded, in his pocket.

Back at home Sir Grandley had the walls of all his rooms covered with other such heads, mounted, not to mention tails and in-between bits.

The people of Clawness were dreadfully upset at the loss of their dragon.

First, because the tourists stopped coming. No more coins at the turnstile, no customers at the fish-and-chip shop, no cars in the car park.

Second, because, very soon, they had a worrying pile of tins and bottles and broken bedsteads and toasters.

Third - and worst - they just plain missed their dear dragon, curled up there above them on the hill, breathing a plume of smoke from time to time, or melting the winter snow with her warm breath.

"There's nae doubt we need a replacement," said Mr Mack the mayor. "Nae doubt at a'."

"But who knows where to find one?" wept his wife.

"I've a notion," said Mr Campbell the dentist.

A year ago, when Gleer seemed to be having trouble munching champagne bottles, which are very thick, Mr Campbell had given her a local anaesthetic, checked all her teeth, and found and mended a broken one with an epoxy filling. While doing this, he had noticed a small cave in the hillside, its entrance usually blocked by dragon. Now he went back, entered the cave, looked about, and returned to the hotel beaming with triumph.

"Look!" he said to Mrs Mack. "If this isn't a dragon's egg I'll swallow my x-ray machine."

The dragon's egg (if that was what it was) weighed more than a sack of coal, though it was no bigger than a teapot. It was rough and lumpy, covered with scales and fossils.

"Maybe we should x-ray it?" suggested Mr Mack. "See what's inside?"

"Och, no! That might hurt the poor wee chick that's in it."

"It wants warmth for hatching," said Mr Campbell. "If you could put it in your bottom oven, Mrs Mack? Dragons are warm-blooded . . ."

They all sighed, thinking of the fine hot draught that used to come down the hill.

The egg was wrapped in flannel and tucked into the warming oven.

"How long do you suppose it will take?" said Mrs Campbell.

"Aweel, that, of course, we don't know. It may take hundreds of years."

Just the same, Mr Campbell dropped in, every six hours or so, to inspect the dragon's egg and turn it over.

"For I've observed that nesting-birds, gannets and guillemots, make a practice of regularly turning their eggs with their beaks," he said. "That way the fledgelings willna hatch lopsided."

He talked to the egg on these visits as well, gave a bit of a hiss, and tapped the shell.

"I heard it said on one o' they educational programmes on the television," he explained, "that you should talk to children before they are born. So they know there's a meaning to the sound of the human voice."

"Aye, indeed? I just hope it hatches soon," said Mr Mack. "For the pile of broken refrigerators is growing higher and higher."

One morning Mrs Mack was very excited.

"I heard a tap! A tap from the oven!"

They pulled out the egg and unwrapped it.

Mr Campbell tapped it with a spoon.

Instantly there came a response from inside. Knock! Knock!

"Who's there?" cried Mr Campbell.

"Maybe I should give it a bit of a tap with my hammer?" suggested Mr Mack. "Or a trifle of help with a hacksaw?"

But Mr Campbell said, "Let nature take its course. We don't want to upset the wee creature."

He brought along some tapes to play to the egg: lions roaring, and crocodiles bellowing.

"For," he said, "the poor orphan is going to grow up without a mother, or any of its ain kind. We must e'en do our best for it."

At last, one midnight, the egg cracked. And then Mr Mack was allowed to give it a gentle tap with his hammer.

The two halves fell apart - they were as thick as telephone directories - and out stepped the smallest dragon anyone had ever seen.

"Ah, bless him, the dear little wean!" cried Mrs Mack. "I shall call him Wee Geordie!"

A dear little wean, Wee Geordie was *not*; less than the length of Mr Campbell's middle finger, he was the ugliest, scrawniest, scaliest, spiniest baby they had ever seen. But he was certainly a dragon; there was no doubt of that. He had the horns, the claws, the wings, the snout, the crest, the scales, the sting in the tail; he even opened his tiny jaws, bellowed a tiny bellow, and puffed a tiny jet of flame.

"Save us, he's ravenous!" said Mrs Campbell. "What at all should we give the little angel?"

"Aweel, his mother was fond of broken glass—"

"I'll just grind up a tonic bottle in the blender," said Mrs Mack.

At first, Wee Geordie was not too sure about eating ground glass. He huffled and snuffled and snarled.

"A touch of the wind, poor lambie," wailed Mrs Campbell.

"Maybe we should melt the glass with a bunsen burner?"

But when the ground glass was mixed

with a drop of brandy, Wee Geordie took it. In fact he consumed three tonic bottles and some marmalade jars. This was plainly the right diet for him. And he began to grow.

Soon he was as big as a cucumber.

Then as long as an umbrella.

Then about the size of a golf bag, but much heavier.

Mr Campbell, and lots of other neighbours, came every day to feed Geordie, sing to him, and play with him.

"Dinna spoil him," warned Mr Mack.

"He has to get accustomed to human company," said Mrs Mack.

Playing with Wee Geordie was a fairly risky occupation. He didn't know his own strength. And his claws were razor-sharp from the start. And his temper was touchy.

"A teenage dragon is an awfu' worry," sighed Mr Mack.

"The sooner he learns to fly, the better," said Mrs Mack. "I'm ne'er a one to grumble - but twenty rugs burned to cinders - and a' the mirrors smashed to smithereens . . ."

When Geordie saw his reflection in a

mirror, he was apt to take it for another dragon.

"I'll teach him to fly," said Mr Campbell, who felt that, as he had found Geordie, he had a duty to turn him into a useful neighbour. "Then, I'm thinking, he won't feel sae fretful and frustrated. He needs the exercise, too."

It is hard to teach a dragon to fly.

Every day, Mr Campbell led Geordie down to the beach, and showed him the gulls and gannets and guillemots, all flying about their business. Geordie snapped at them, but he didn't catch on to the idea of taking to the air himself.

"Look, Geordie! Do like me! Do like this!" And Mr Campbell ran along the sand, flapping his arms.

Geordie stared at him, bored. If a dragon can scowl, he scowled.

The town children wanted to help. But Mr Campbell forbade this.

"He might gobble you up, not meaning any harm, ye ken."

For Geordie was now as big as a minibus,

and his temper was worsening.

"Och, I'm afeard we spoiled him, among us!" lamented Mrs Mack.

Day after day, Mr Campbell pounded up and down the beach, and Geordie lumbered along behind him, puzzled and glum, as if he wondered why he was obliged to waste his time in this way.

"*Look*, Geordie, *flap*! Flap like this!"

Geordie's wings hung sulkily at his sides. They were growing, *he* was growing, but he never seemed to conceive the idea of using them.

Mr Campbell was growing thinner and thinner.

"He's just worn out!" worried his wife.

And then - one day - triumph!

It was a windy spring morning, quite a few tourists had turned up (news of the replacement dragon had been filtering around the countryside) and, all of a sudden, Geordie, as he trundled heavily behind Mr Campbell, had the impulse to lift up his wings and give them a waft.

Up he went like a kite - soared across the sky, swung and swooped and swam in the air, greatly alarming the gulls, then floated down to settle, just as his mother had done, coiled around the mountain top.

Only, on the way, as mischance would have it, he swallowed half a dozen tourists who were eating their picnic on the hillside.

After a week Mr Mack said to Mr

Campbell, "This willna do, you know. Twenty-four tourists, and the postman on his bike. Publicity for the town it may be, but not the kind we want."

Sadly, Mr Campbell agreed.

"I'm thinking we'd best write to Sir Grandley Upshott."

The knight was sent for. (Fortunately his address was in the hotel guest book.)

When Sir Grandley saw the dragon coiled on the hilltop, a gleam came into his eye.

"A six-pointer! Look at those horns."

"I should mention he's no' so easy-natured as his mother," warned Mrs Mack.

"I'll put on all my armour," said Sir Grandley.

Shining in helmet and shield, breast-plate and cuisses, he walked up the hill, electric sword in hand.

And Wee Geordie swallowed him in one snap, whoomphfsch!

"Oh, bless me, what'll we do the noo?" said Mrs Campbell.

But swallowing a knight in full armour

had been too much for Wee Geordie's teenage digestive system; he developed hiccups and heartburn and that was the end of him.

Now they are advertising in the *Clawness Weekly Herald*: "Loving dragon required. Fare paid from anywhere."

So - if you are a loving dragon - you know where to go.

MILO'S NEW WORD

When Uncle Claud Armitage came back from the island of Eridu, he brought some problems for his niece and nephews.

Climbing stiffly off the train (for Uncle Claud was quite an old man) he started the walk up Station Road to his brother's house. But he soon noticed that he was being followed.

Pit-pat, pit-pat went the footsteps behind him in the dusk.

Uncle Claud stepped into a phone box and dialled his brother's number.

Outside the lighted box, in the shadows, something waited and listened.

"Hallo?" piped a little voice in Uncle Claud's ear.

"Hallo? Is that Mark or Harriet? Listen, quickly, there's no time to lose. I want to tell you a tremendously important mathematical secret - the greatest discovery since Euclid—"

He went on talking very fast. After a while he said: "Did you get that?"

"Hallo?" said the little voice again.

Behind Uncle Claud the door was softly opening. He looked round - just too late. He felt the lightest possible touch on his arm. Next minute his fingers curled up and turned black. They had become claws. His arms stretched out, flattened, and became leathery wings. Uncle Claud shrank. With a whirr and a flip, he soared away into the dark-blue evening sky, where one star had just flashed out, ahead of all the others.

Uncle Claud had turned into a bat.

At the Armitage house, Mark was setting the table for supper while Harriet made scrambled eggs. Their parents were out at a Village Green Improvement Society meeting in the church hall. Their young brother Milo was on the bottom stair, building a castle out of telephone directories.

"Who rang up?" Harriet asked, as Mark came back from the front hall.

"I dunno," he said. "I got there just too late. Milo had picked up the phone."

"Milo!" called Harriet. "You're a naughty boy! You know you aren't supposed to play with the phone."

"Hallo!" said Milo. It was his word this week. Last week his word had been 'Perhaps'. Milo used one word at a time.

"It's funny he's so fond of the phone," said Mark. "Seeing he's so slow at learning to talk."

"Oh well," said Harriet, "I expect who-ever it was will phone again."

But the phone did not ring again, and soon Mr and Mrs Armitage came home, arguing about the village green.

"A ring of poplars would be nice."

"A ring of poplars would be *silly*."

When they were halfway through their scrambled egg, the doorbell rang. "Who can it be, so late?" said Mrs Armitage. "See who it is, Harriet, there's a love."

Harriet came back from the front hall, her eyes popping with excitement.

"It's a man who says he's from the Department of Security and Secrets."

"I suppose I'd better go," said her father, sighing.

The man at the front door had silver-rimmed glasses, a short black beard, a soft black hat, and a long black umbrella. He looked very cross.

"It's a matter of extreme secrecy," he said. "Half an hour ago a phone call was made to this house. It should not have been made. I must speak to whoever answered the phone."

"Oh, that's all right," Harriet told him. "It was only our brother Milo."

"I must see him at once!"

Harriet looked at her father, who shrugged, and said, "Let the gentleman see Milo. Then he'll know there's nothing to worry about." He explained to the caller, "Milo's only two, and a backward talker. He's much too young to understand government secrets."

Harriet went and fetched Milo. He was in his pyjamas, sucking a bedtime bottle of milk.

"You see," said Mr Armitage to the visitor. "There's absolutely no cause for—"

His words came to a sudden stop. For the man in the doorway had pointed his umbrella at Milo, who turned grey, sprouted a trunk and tiny tusks, and slipped from Harriet's limp grip on to the floor.

"No cause to worry *now*," snapped the visitor, turned on his heel, and strode away into the dark.

Harriet said to Mark, who came out of the kitchen, "That man has changed Milo into a baby elephant."

"Oh dear," said Mr Armitage. "I'm afraid your mother won't be pleased."

Next morning Harriet and her father went to ask the advice of Mr Moondew, a retired alchemist who had lately come to live in the village, and was very friendly and useful in the Village Improvement Society.

Mark stayed at home, rigging up a harness for Milo. It had struck him that his brother, who seemed a very good-natured little elephant, might be a great help in the garden.

Mrs Armitage stayed at home because she was upset. She had been knitting a new blue sweater for Milo, and could not decide whether to go on with it.

Crossing the village green, Harriet and her father were surprised to see six red phone-boxes standing in a row under the big lime tree.

"British Telecom's selling 'em off," explained Mr Pullie, the street-cleaner, leaning on his broom. "A foreign gent, he made an offer for 'em. Going to convert them to fancy bathroom showers, I heard. Paid a fancy price for 'em. BT's going to put new plain-glass boxes in Station Road and Grove Lane and Mistletoe Crescent and Holly Ride and Copse Alley and Vicar's Way."

"Shame," said Harriet, who liked the red phone boxes.

"I'd no idea there were so many call-boxes in the village," said her father.

They found Mr Moondew clipping his front hedge. He was most interested to hear that Milo had been turned into an elephant. He asked a lot of questions.

"You say he had answered the telephone shortly before? You don't know who was calling?"

"No," said Harriet, "but the man from the Department of Secrets seemed very cross about it."

"I'd like to come and take a look at your brother."

Crossing the green again, they saw two men by the phone boxes. One was their visitor of last night. They could hear him saying angrily, "Those boxes have *got* to be moved by Saturday."

"Well, guv," said the other man, who was Mr Miller, of Miller's Removals, "sorry and all that, but my trucks are busy till then."

"Sir!" said Harriet's father to the man from the DOS, "you had no right to change my younger son into an elephant. I must insist that you reverse the process. At once!"

But the bearded man, without troubling to answer Mr Armitage, took his hat off and flung it on the ground. It turned into a Rolls Royce, and he jumped into it and drove off.

"How rude of him!" said Mr Armitage.

But Mr Moondew said, "You are lucky that he didn't change you into a toad. That man wasn't from any government department. I know him from college days. He is a powerful warlock from the ghost island of Eridu."

"Why," cried Harriet, "that's where Uncle Claud was going for his holiday. He was supposed to come back yesterday."

"Now things are becoming clear," said Mr Moondew. "Perhaps it was your Uncle Claud who rang last night? And our bearded friend (his name is Logroth) wanted to prevent him. What is your brother's profession?" he asked Mr Armitage.

"He's a professor of mathematics."

"Aha! The ghost island of Eridu is full of runes, and mathematical secrets—"

"And now the only person who knows the secret is Milo," said Harriet. "And *he* certainly won't tell . . ."

"But the knowledge, the secret, is still there, stored inside his youthful mind," said Mr Moondew. "But this gives me an idea as to what can be done for him—"

They had reached the Armitage garden where Milo, sturdy and good-natured, was pulling the big garden roller, encouraged by Mark, and watched anxiously by his mother, who was waiting to feed him a large dish-tub of bread and milk.

"Dear me, a most handsome small beast," said Mr Moondew. "You are quite certain you do not prefer to keep him like this?"

"Quite certain!" said Mrs Armitage indignantly.

"So. What you must do is this. Each day at dusk, when the star Hesperus first shines in the sky, you must place him in one of those red phone boxes. Each night a different one. For, from one of them was the secret message sent, and the echo of it will remain in the box, only to be heard by Milo. Hearing it a second time will change him back. But he must be in the box *just* at that instant, when the star shines. For so must it have been last night."

"Suppose it's raining?"

"Makes no difference if the time is correct. But I must warn you—"

"Yes, what?" said Mrs Armitage nervously, clasping Milo's little trunk, which had twined confidingly into her pocket.

"Standing in the right box, he will at once change back into your charming little son. But if it is *not* the right one, he will merely double in size."

"Lucky he's not very big now," said Mark thoughtfully.

"Yes - but suppose we keep getting the wrong one - and he doubles again - and *again* - oh well, we'll just have to hope for the best." Mr Armitage measured the size of his small son with a thoughtful eye. "Anyhow, most obliging of you, Moondew."

That evening, just at dusk, Mark and Harriet led their young brother out on to the village green. The sky was clear and a pale duck-egg blue; their father had calculated that Hesperus was due to sparkle out in precisely four minutes' time. But when they came to within a few metres of the call-box at the end of the row of six, a large flock of savage magpies dropped down from the lime tree above, pecking and squawking and flapping, dashing fiercely into their faces.

"Hmn, yes, thought we might get a bit of interference," said Mark.

He slipped a handful of firework

sparklers from his pocket, lit them, and tossed them to the ground, where they fizzed and spat and hopped about, and flung up showers of heat and glitter and puffs of yellow smoke. The magpies made off, screeching angrily.

"Now, quick, you hold open the door and I'll shove him in," said Mark.

This done, they stood with their backs to the glass door and arms across their eyes, in case the magpies wanted to make a come-back. But the magpies had taken fright and were seen no more.

Sadly, it was not the right box. Hesperus flashed out in the sky, bright as the fire-works, the puzzled Milo was told that he could come out, but all that had happened was that he had doubled in size. Now, he was as big as a Shetland pony.

"Never mind, my duck. Better luck tomorrow, perhaps," comforted Harriet, twining her arm into Milo's trunk. "Come on home. Muesli and buns for supper."

"He'll need quite a lot." Mark looked anxiously from his brother to the row of phone booths, counting on his fingers. "Monday today. By Saturday - if we keep choosing the wrong box - it'll be no joke squeezing him in . . ."

Next evening the interference was caused by snakes: large, thick, black ones as long as bean-poles, who appeared, hissing disagreeably, out of the village pond, and twined themselves all around the second phone-box.

Elephants can't stand snakes. Milo trumpeted and reared, and seemed likely to panic and bolt into the next county. But Mark had been prepared for trouble. He had a large can of fixative, used for drawing classes at school. He sprayed the fixative over the snakes, who became quite stiff with disgust, and shot back into the pond.

"I'll never go near it again," shuddered Harriet.

But - alas - today's box was still not the right one; Hesperus shone out, but Milo simply doubled in size, and could only just be dragged out of the booth, levered on each side by garden shovels.

Next evening, in front of the row of phone-boxes, they found a dragon. But Harriet knew all about dragons; she ran to the village shop and returned dragging a laundry-basket full of eggs. These the dragon was happy to eat, whipping them up one at a time with his long forked tongue. He took no more notice of Mark, Harriet, or Milo.

They had brought a big flask of vegetable oil, and they poured it all over Milo before pushing him into the box. It made him very slippery.

"It's lucky he's so patient and good," panted Harriet, wiping oil from her eyes, her arms, her hair, her jacket, her teeth and her shoes, while the Evening Star came softly into the clear green sky.

That was their only luck. Milo did not change back into their young brother, but merely doubled in size, stretching and bending the phone box into a barrel shape.

"Having the box like this," panted Mark, hauling on his brother's leg, "at least makes it easier to slide him out."

TELEPHONE

"I'm afraid the person who bought the boxes isn't going to be pleased. There, there, baby! All better now," to Milo, who was a bit disgruntled.

On the fourth evening rain poured down from a thick and soggy sky; Mark and Harriet, having carefully checked Hesperus's coming-out time on their watches, were discouraged, as they led the whimpering Milo across the green, to see that the fourth phone-box was all wrapped in cobwebs, and when they came up to it, a fat black spider, big as a barrel, slid down on a line from the tree above, gnashed its teeth at them, pulled open the phone-box door with its pincers, and nipped inside.

"Oh dear. Now what'll we do? I hate spiders," said Harriet, and Milo plainly shared her feelings, for he trumpeted dismally.

"But it's simple. There's no rule about which box we try," said Mark. "The spider's welcome to that one, if he wants it. We'll put Milo in this one."

And he poured oil over his brother and

stuffed him (with difficulty) into the fifth phone-box.

At that very moment a black cloud on the horizon drifted away. Hesperus blazed out as if sponged clean, and a whole lot of things happened all together.

Milo changed back from a medium-sized elephant into a small boy in blue-striped pyjamas, clutching a bottle of milk, and covered from head to foot in salad oil.

The huge spider exploded, shattering the phone box it occupied, as well as the ones on either side, with a tremendous, echoing clap of sound.

Something fell heavily on Harriet from above, and she let out a yell, thinking that it must be another spider.

But it turned out to be her Uncle Claud, who was in a dazed state.

Soon quite a large crowd of people had gathered on the green, including Mr Moondew, Mr and Mrs Armitage, and the village policeman, Sergeant Frith.

"*Milo!* Milo! My own, precious, oily boy!" exclaimed Mrs Armitage, and hugged the slippery Milo, who was wailing with fright at all these happenings.

"A most successful result of your efforts," Mr Moondew congratulated Mark and his sister.

"But where in the world did Uncle Claud come from?" wondered Harriet.

"That, we shall perhaps know when your uncle recovers," said Mr Moondew.

But Uncle Claud was no help. When he recovered his wits he could recall nothing of his trip to Eridu, nothing of what he learned there, nothing of what happened after he got home.

When Sergeant Frith went, rather gingerly, to inspect the exploded spider, he found that it seemed to have turned into the man from the Department of Security and Secrets - or, more properly, Logroth, the warlock from the ghost island of Eridu. He had fainted. But, while they were waiting for an ambulance, he sat up, pulled off his black beard, flung it on the ground, where it became a Rolls Royce, and he drove away in it at top speed.

He was never seen again - except, presumably, in the ghost island of Eridu.

On the following day the six battered red telephone-boxes were found to have changed overnight into poplar trees, a ring of them, growing in the centre of the village green.

Mr Armitage said they looked silly.

British Telecom announced that they were not prepared to replace all six phone-boxes. A single plain glass one in Station Road would be quite sufficient, they said.

"But what about the secret mathematical message?" said Harriet to Mr Moondew, who had called in and was playing chess with Uncle Claud. "What about the information, the important secret - whatever it was - that Uncle Claud brought back from the ghost island of Eridu?"

"We'll have to wait for that," said Mr Moondew. "That information is locked inside your young brother's head. Sooner or later - when he has learned to speak, and knows the use of letters and numbers and decimals and logarithms - he will be able to tell us what it was. Won't you, Milo?"

Milo looked up from the carpet, where he was building a nuclear power station with telephone directories, and grinned.

"Elephant," he said.

It was his new word.

THE FURIOUS TREE

Long ago, more than a thousand years ago, there lived a wicked lord. His name was Sir Gaston du Gard. The two things he enjoyed most in the world were fighting battles and hunting wild animals. The King, his over-lord, gave him, as a reward for fighting in various battles, the hand of a wealthy heiress, Dame Isabelle de Neuve, whose properties included nine villages, nine churches, and hundreds of acres of rich cornfields and grassy meadows. She was a happy, laughing lady, but she never laughed again after she heard that she was to marry Sir Gaston. She hated him, but nobody dared disobey the King, and so the wedding took place. The bride's wide lands passed to

Sir Gaston, and she was obliged to live in his castle, Grim Gard, which stood in the middle of a wood. Lady Isabelle's sunny meadows, her golden cornfields, fertile pastures, lush vineyards, water-mills, farm-houses, sheepfolds, dovecotes and the nine villages all lay to the west of this wood.

"Now," said Sir Gaston, the very moment the marriage ceremony had been performed, and all the papers had been signed, "now I shall tear down all those villages and farms and churches; I shall plant a new forest, which, by the side of the one I own already, will make it the largest stretch of wild wood in this whole kingdom; and I shall spend all my days in it, hunting (unless the King needs me for a battle, of course)."

Lady Isabelle was horrified. "Pull down my cottages? Plant trees in my cornfields? But where will the people go? There are nine whole villages! Almost a thousand people will be homeless!"

"Then they will just have to march off and find themselves new homes," said Sir

Gaston, and he set his men-at-arms to work directly, pulling down houses and chasing people out of their cottages. The householders were not allowed to take their pigs, goats, cows, and poultry with them, for Sir Gaston said these belonged to the Lord of the Manor.

"But where will they go?" said Lady Isabelle. "How will they live?"

"What do I care about that?" said Sir Gaston.

It was autumn when the people were turned out of their homes. A cold wind with some flakes of snow in it whistled over the ridges that lay to the east of the forest. The householders begged and prayed, they groaned and cursed, as they were driven out of their cottages, but the men-at-arms took no notice; they were from another country and it was nothing to them if families with small children, or old people who could hardly hobble along, were thrust out of their own kitchens or driven from their own firesides. Already as the villagers trudged miserably along the road leading to nowhere, the soldiers behind them were knocking stone from stone, setting fire to thatch, and herding the poultry and cattle into the Lord's barns and rick-yards.

Sir Gaston came down into one of the villages at dusk one day to make sure that his orders were being carried out. He rode a big red war-horse, and his thick red hair streamed out behind him as he galloped between buildings now half-demolished, whose trampled gardens were beginning to be crusted with silver by frost. Above them on one side the evening star rode clear and greenish in the pale sky; over the chimneys on the other side of the street a nameless flash of light, a comet, trailed a speckled, shining plume behind it like a witch's broom in the rusty western heavens.

Several of the villagers made the sign of the cross when they caught sight of this new portent in the sky; others abused it, in whispers.

"What can you expect but misfortune, with that wicked thing sliding across above us? Where does it come from? Why was it never here before? No wonder such troubles have fallen on us! That new flashing thing must have come from the Bad Place. It belongs to the Red Beast."

That was their name for Sir Gaston.

But his feelings about the comet were just the reverse.

"It has brought me luck!" he gloated. "Ever since it came climbing up into the western sky, my luck has mounted and risen. It has red hair, too, just like mine." (For the comet's long double plume, which trailed behind it, like the beam thrown by a lantern, was reddish in colour.)

At the far end of the village, Sir Gaston overtook the tail of the long, miserable procession of expelled villagers, carrying bundles and boxes, with tearful children perched on their shoulders, and growling dogs trotting alongside, and howling, mewling cats in baskets.

Most of the people were too afraid of Sir Gaston, even now, even when things seemed as bad as they could, to say out loud what they felt in their hearts, but there were some whispered curses, and a few fists were shaken, as the Lord of the Manor cantered alongside and glanced down at them without much interest. To him they seemed just human rubbish, sweepings that needed to be shoved out of sight, before he could have his lands all to himself.

On the whole, Sir Gaston disliked people; he had been a younger son who cordially hated his elder brother, and it was only by the good fortune of that elder brother happening to fall over a cliff that Sir Gaston inherited his title and property. How the brother had come to fall, nobody inquired.

"That's good, clear out, hurry up, get away from here, you ugly rabble. Get you all gone, scum that you are!" he bawled at the trudging people. "Soon there will be green oak trees growing here, and empty woodland rides, and only the rustling of red deer or wild boar in the brambles, nothing but the sound of my hunting horn to break the silence."

"And a fine peace, a fine silence that will

be, you heartless man!" hissed a fierce voice, and a tall old woman stepped aside from the sad procession and faced Sir Gaston with burning eyes and clenched fists. "And when you are enjoying that same peace, when you listen to the rustle of your red deer and wild boar in the brambles, let you sometimes spare a thought for the folk whose bones lie mouldering on the cold ground because you took their homes from them, and their livelihood. Wretch! Villain! Hateful despoiler!"

"Quiet, you old hag!" exclaimed Sir Gaston. "How dare you speak to your Lord in such a way? Not that anybody cares what you say! Be off! Get away with you to perdition, or wherever you are going!" And he called for his men-at-arms to give the old woman a beating, and hurry her on her way. But they seemed reluctant to obey his command.

"See, she's the wise woman of the village, my Lord," one of them apologised. "They say she has uncommon powers. Best not to cross her."

The old woman walked to the head of Sir Gaston's charger, who snorted and reared. She laid a strong hand on his bridle, to calm him, and went on fiercely addressing his rider.

"Oh yes! Yes indeed! You may sound your hunting horn, my fine Lord! And long may the sound of that horn echo in the forest! And long may you gallop through those empty, silent glades! Until that red-plumed comet that rides up there in the heaven has travelled to the farthest reaches of black space, and returned to our skies again, until it has made a hundred hundred journeys - for so long may your black soul go questing through the universe and never, never find what it seeks. Hunting! Yes, you will hunt! A merry hunt to you indeed, my valiant huntsman!"

And with a hazel wand, which she held in her left hand, the old woman gave Sir Gaston's horse a tap which, gentle though it seemed, made the beast scream aloud and go bounding sideways across the small plundered gardens and between the empty ruined cottages.

"Seize that old hag!" he shouted, jerking on the reins of his horse until it reared again. "Take her and nail her to a tree!"

But the men-at-arms, running to obey him, stared up and down the trampled street in puzzlement; suddenly there was no old woman to be seen.

Only a voice, and the sound of angry laughter, passed along the village street between the ruined houses.

"Yes, you will hunt! Yes, you will travel,

my Lord! You will travel, travel, travel, travel, travel . . ."

"Grab her!" shouted Sir Gaston, fighting to control his frantic horse. "Catch her and bind her and nail her to that tree."

He pointed to a great chestnut tree which grew at the far end of the village. But they could not catch her. The old woman was nowhere to be found.

And the soldiers crossed themselves, sweating with fear, staring at the tree. It was of huge growth, a hundred metres high, with a wrinkled, twisted trunk, and few leaves left on its bare branches, after the autumn storms. Plainly, in the course of its long life, it had survived many and terrible tempests, for the top of its trunk and at least half its branches had been broken off, and only shattered, sharp-pointed fragments remained, extended outwards from the trunk like begging hands. The top of the trunk ended in a point, like a witch's hat, and on one side, below this hat-like shape, was a great gap in the side of the tree, like an open mouth. Indeed the whole tree strangely resembled a tall, angry woman, stretching out her battered arms and screaming with rage.

"Find the old hag and nail her to that tree!" again commanded Sir Gaston.

"But, my Lord - she's gone! We can't see her anywhere. And - and - and - the tree—"

But none of the men dared tell Sir Gaston the terribly strange thing about the tree. Which was that, ten minutes ago, it had not been there.

By now the forlorn trail of villagers had disappeared into the gathering dusk; only their sad voices could be heard faintly across the fields, which would soon be planted with new trees.

And that other new tree, which looked so old and battered, grew as if it had always grown there at the far end of the village street. But Sir Gaston paid no heed to it. One tree was of no interest to him. He turned his horse and rode slowly in the opposite direction - as if, for the first time in his vigorous life, he did not greatly care what he did next.

Some months later, Sir Gaston's wife bore him a son. And in doing so the Lady Isabelle died. Her ladies-in-waiting and the people in Grim Gard whispered that it was because of the old woman's curse that she had died; that nothing went right for Sir Gaston since that day.

Sir Gaston never troubled himself to marry again. The boy, his son, was christened John, but his father took little notice of him and gave him only sour looks and harsh words, for their characters were so completely different that nothing John did pleased his father.

Like his mother, John had a lucky, happy way with him; plants grew if he tended them, sick animals throve under his care, the sun shone on his birthday, he never got lost in the forest, learned his lessons with ease, and could always find his path back to a special plant or tree or favourite spot in the forest.

On his thirteenth birthday John went to his father and said, "I am leaving Grim Gard, Father. I am going to go my own way from now on."

"*Go, then*! And good riddance to you!" growled Sir Gaston. "What do I care where you choose to spend your days? I dare say you will starve soon enough and then be glad to come whining back."

"No. I shall not starve," said John; and he slung a pack over his shoulder, took a hazel staff in his hand, gave a last pat to the castle watchdog, and went whistling on his way.

"How will you make your living?" called his father after him with a sneer.

"By luck," John answered.

And it was by luck indeed that he lived, for his sharp eyes, always so keen to spot an orchid, or a rare bird's nest, or a weasel crossing the track, or a vixen with her brood of cubs hidden under a clump of fern, were easily able to catch sight of things that people had dropped or lost. As he trudged along the pathway John would detect the gleam of a shoe-buckle, or a penny, or a knife, a brooch or a stirrup, small things, but he could usually exchange them for a crust of bread or a bowl of soup.

But mostly it was cast horseshoes that John picked up - for in those days the roads were all mud, or clay, or sand, or pebbles; and it was a long way from one blacksmith to the next, and if a horse lost a shoe, there was nothing to be done but limp on without it to the next village.

Often, by the end of a lucky day, John would be the richer by nine or ten horseshoes, if the road he took was a well-travelled one, and he would stop at the forge in the last village on his day's journey, and offer the smith his haul of horseshoes in exchange for a share of supper and a night's lodging. Sometimes he might stay for a week or two and help out in the forge, if it was a busy one, for he soon grew handy at the blacksmith's trade; often he received an invitation to stay for the rest of his life, since he was a friendly fellow, and good company, and had a stock of songs and stories besides; but he always said no to that.

"Why do you never stop for long in one place?" he was sometimes asked, and to that he would say, "Because of my father. Because he did a mortal wrong to so many people. Because it makes my heart ache, night and day, to think of it. Because of that I can never rest."

"But your father's crime is not yours."

"We are all in this world together," John would say to that, and next morning he would be off at dawn, whistling on his way.

By those who met him in the road he was given the name of Horseshoe John, and, after a while, people began to say that he was a luck-bringer, that often, if you met him, on the heath, or in a market-place, or crossing a ford, some piece of good fortune would come to you soon after.

They sang a song about him, perhaps one that he had made up himself.

"Horseshoe John, Horseshoe John
Carries the weight of his father's wrong
Broke is broke and can't be mended
What's begun can never be ended . . ."

But what became of Sir Gaston? Daily, after John left the castle, he grew gloomier and more silent; he rode out hunting every morning, as was his custom, but seemed to take less and less pleasure in the chase. His servants and soldiers agreed among themselves that he seemed to be *listening* all the time - listening to something, perhaps distant voices that nobody else could hear. One day he galloped off by himself into the woods and did not come back; his horse returned at nightfall, riderless, but though a search was made for his master through the forest, far and near, Sir Gaston could not be found anywhere. So a month went by, and then, much to everybody's amazement, he was discovered lying at the foot of a great old chestnut tree which had once stood at the end of a busy village street. Now it was in the middle of the forest, surrounded by new young growth.

Mysteriously, Sir Gaston appeared to have died of *hunger*, though he lay by a track where people passed daily.

After Sir Gaston's death, the title and property should have gone to his son, and a search was made for Horseshoe John throughout the country; but though many people came forward to say they had seen him quite recently - or not long ago - or last year - or the year before that - nobody could be found who knew where he was at the present time; and, in fact, he was never seen again. In the meantime the lawyers argued about the inheritance, the trees in the forest grew taller and taller, and Grim Gard fell down, for nobody cared to live there, or had the right to.

Ten years went by - then a hundred - then five hundred - then a thousand . . .

But the story of Horseshoe John remained alive in that country; legends were told of him, songs were sung; a man's grandfather had met him along the roads, a great-uncle had seen him on the common, a neighbour had heard a snatch of his song on the village green, a cousin had heard that a smith in a distant hamlet told a tale of how a good-natured fellow had dropped in and offered half-a-dozen horseshoes in exchange for a plate of stew and a doss-down in the stable. So the tales of Horseshoe John remained alive.

And Sir Gaston? He was remembered

only when the red comet returned - which it did every ninety-nine years. "The Red Beast has come back to revisit the scene of his crime," country people said, looking at the trail of red light in the western sky. And they would shake their heads and add, "*He* won't rest for many a hundred years yet! Not while the Furious Tree still grows in the wood." And the forest planted by Sir Gaston came to be known as Furious Wood.

Here, now, was another mystery. After the death of Sir Gaston, after he had been laid in the graveyard alongside the Lady Isabelle, the great ruined tree, at the foot of which Sir Gaston's body had been found, was suddenly gone from its place - as suddenly and unaccountably as it had come. The ground was undisturbed. Patches of wood-garlic and wood-sorrel and wild violets grew peacefully on that spot as if they had always done so. No sign or trace showed that a huge tree had once stood there.

But yet, after that, from time to time, a wayfarer in the wood might catch a glimpse of the Furious Tree - perhaps at the far end of a glade, or in a distant dell. And often, according to these tales, there would appear to be a man standing at the foot of the tree, a man dressed in dark clothes, with his head bowed low, a man who shivered and trembled, rocked back and forth and wrung his hands, as if he begged and prayed for mercy. No one doubted that this was Sir Gaston, still serving his long sentence. He was only to be seen when the comet came near, never when it had gone off into the distant realms of space.

After a thousand years, new times arrived. There were more people in the land. Towns grew bigger, and spread over the open fields. Men lived longer, and wanted larger houses for their families. On the edge of the Furious Wood a town called New Nineham had grown up, a town of fifty-thousand inhabitants. And, these days, the wood had come to be called Furry Wood. But children in the local schools still told stories about Horseshoe John, and the Wicked Lord, and the Furious Tree.

Now a new highway was to be made, slicing through the forest; and a thousand new homes were to be put up in the crescent of land between the town and the new motorway.

A group of local people were protesting about this plan. They said that it was wrong to cut a road through the forest, which was ancient woodland, preserved just exactly as it had been since before the beginnings of history.

But there were plenty of others who took a different view. Some said that the forest was rooted in evil and misery, that people had been forced from their homes, people had died of hunger and cold, to make a rich baron's playground. Such a wood did not deserve to remain, was their view, it should be cut down and forgotten. Far better build new homes there, and house people who would be happy to pay for them and live there with their families. Lady Isabelle, these people said, would be glad to know that her lands were at last being put to good use, for the benefit of many, and not kept for the pleasure of one lonely, angry man, who passed his days chasing wild boar and red deer. (It was mostly the older people who felt this way, the kind who would be able to buy the houses and live in them.)

The young people were against the road and the new housing developments, or, at least, wanted them somewhere else. They wanted the forest preserved as it had been for so many years. These young ones built themselves tree-houses in the threatened stretch of woodland, or they tunnelled under the ground where the new road was to be laid, to make it unsafe. The young people gave themselves new names, Nutkin and Piglet and Hobyah and Turpie and Honest Jim and Horseshoe Johnnie.

The boy who called himself Horseshoe Johnnie had built himself a fine tree-house in a huge old chestnut tree which the local school children called the Furry Tree. It had grown there as long as any of them could remember, or their parents before them; it stretched out broken branches like beseeching arms, it was all gashed and smashed from storms in many winters past; a hole in its trunk near the top looked like a wide, angry mouth which seemed to yell defiance at the developers coming with their bulldozers and their chainsaws.

Horseshoe Johnnie's tree-cabin, made from brushwood and hedge-clippings, had been tucked and rammed into the gap between the two broken arm-branches; there was a hollow in the massive old trunk behind him where he could keep his books and food; he had a waterproof cover and he had nailed a chain to the tree, to which, when the bulldozers and cranes came at him, he planned to fasten himself with handcuffs so that it would need a hacksaw to cut him loose.

Meanwhile he was very snug up there, writing his poems and singing his songs, and waiting for the giant crane to come and snap at him. He would give it as good as he got, he reckoned; no crane would easily get the better of him.

"Horseshoe Johnnie," he sang, up in his tree:

"Horseshoe Johnnie, walking lonely
Bearing the weight of your father's wrong
One day, some day, the gates will open
The lost will be found
What's broke will mend
You'll find a place where you belong . . ."

Perhaps Johnnie fell asleep while he sang? For he knew that, after a while, he seemed to be woken by the sound of a telephone ringing. And he knew that he had not brought a mobile phone with him into the tree-house. (He did have one, but had sold it to buy the length of chain.)

However, half-asleep still, he said, "Hello? Who's there?"

"John," a voice answered him. "This is John."

"John? Who's John? How can you be John? *I* am John!"

"Look down," the voice said.

Johnnie looked down - or thought that he looked down, from his high-perched nest. The moon and the stars were bright, the comet shone rustily, crossing low in the western sky. Down at the foot of his great home-made tree Johnnie could see a man in dark clothes, bent over as if in great pain, kneeling on the ground.

"Who is that man?" Johnnie whispered. Though he thought he knew.

"Never mind his name. He is sorry for what he did. All his sorrow, though, cannot right the wrong. Nothing can ever do that. But he can go on, he can do better. He need not spend his time for ever bewailing what is gone. Better build bridges, go forward, make new frames for new lives."

"But," said Johnnie - and now he believed he knew to whom he was talking, "what about *her*?"

"Her?"

"She, the tree, the wise woman, is not she the one who has been hounding him through space all this while? And isn't it just as bad," Johnnie suggested hesitantly, "just as bad to blame as to be blamed? Doesn't it hurt you? Make you feel just as bad as the other person?"

"Yes. That's true. The only way to deal

with guilt or grief is to share it. Let the wind carry it away." And the other sang:

"I'm Horseshoe John, I sing for my bread
Carry the weight of the world on my head
Sing for my supper, talk to trees
Live at ease
All my goods I share
Sorrow, difficulty, glory, air
You may share these, if you please!"

And he said, "Let them build the town, John, if they must; some other forest will grow up somewhere else."

Johnnie looked down again, and now the man in dark clothes was gone. But in the man's place Johnnie was dismayed to see a truck, which had come stealing along silently over the forest floor on its caterpillar treads, and was now unfolding and un-telescoping its crane, length by spindly length. . .

"Oh, John, look! They planned to take us by surprise. But just a moment - I must lock myself to the chain—"

"Never mind the chain, Johnnie. You don't need that. We can take *them* by surprise - watch now—"

A patch of pale-pink sky in the east showed where the sun would soon slide from behind the trees.

The crane stretched up slowly against this pale radiance, black and skeletal like a spider building its web upwards, defying the law of gravity. The men working the crane were so busy getting it into position that for a while they paid no attention to anything else. But when they did finally look about them they let out yelps of surprise.

"Where's the *tree* gone?"

"Where's it got to?"

"It was right here just now - wasn't it?"

"A tree can't just vanish?"

"This one just did!"

The tree was certainly gone. In a patch of bluebells, growing where it had been, a boy sat on the ground. He had a chain buckled to his wrist by a handcuff. He was smiling broadly.

"Have you got a hacksaw?" he said.

"*Where did the tree go*? Don't tell us it wasn't here just now! And who were you talking to, up there, just now? We heard you! Where's the other fellow?"

"I was talking to my friends. They've gone - somewhere else. They have other things to do now. Thanks, mate." as one of the men unlocked his handcuffs. "Would this piece of chain be any use to you?"

And the boy walked off, singing,
"Horseshoe John, what'll you do
When there isn't a horse and there isn't a shoe?
I'll stroll through sunshine, stride through storm,
And look for luck in another form!"

THE MYSTERIOUS MEADOW

Old Mrs Lazarus had died, aged ninety-four. For the last sixty years she had owned Fox Hill Farm, up above Highbury Village. Now her family had all come together - or most of them - to attend her funeral, to hear her will read, and to learn what was to become of the property. Fox Hill Farm covered several hundred acres, over the slope of Highbury Hill, and any estate so close to London was now very valuable indeed.

"It's a wonder she hung on to it for so long," big fat Saul Wodge, one of the grandsons over from Chicago, was saying to his cousin Mark Briskitt, a professor from Manchester. Saul owned nine Fun Parks, scattered all over America, and was about to open a tenth.

"Granny Lazarus grew wonderful crops - parsley, basil, sunflower seeds. She and Uncle Tod were into organic farming long ago, before the rest of the country had even heard of it. They were selling to big hotels and supermarkets."

"No wonder she wanted to be buried under a tree."

"*Very* peculiar - not very nice at all!" said Petunia Wodge, Saul's wife. "Buried under a *tree*? What kind of interment is *that*, I ask you?"

The ceremony had taken place under a young beech tree, one of a narrow belt of beeches forming a windbreak between a ploughed field and a piece of rough down-land pasture which stretched alongside Highbury Common.

Little Rickie Wodge, youngest son of the great-great-grandchildren, had already found blackberries scattered over the brambles bordering the Common, and his cheeks were stained purple.

"*Rickie*! Come back out of that! What

ever have you found? You'll poison yourself!"

Rickie's mother Lara was in Chicago, nursing his six-week-old sister. Petunia, Rickie's grandmother, took off after him like a fury, but she wore shiny black shoes with three-inch heels and a tight lavender-coloured skirt; there was no possible way she could catch up with him as he bounded about, faster than a fire-cracker, fizzing with glee. Brought up in an apartment on the twenty-first floor, he had never seen so much grass in his life.

Forty grown-up children were discussing the will. Sarah Lazarus had lived so long that her three sons and two daughters had died before her.

"*Two acres* to each grandchild! Of their own choice! How in the name of reason is that ever going to be sorted out? It will need half a dozen computers. And how are we going to find everybody?"

One of Sarah's sons, Luke, had moved to Buenos Aires and had six children. None of these had turned up at the funeral.

"It's going to take twenty years to settle the question of who owns every different bit," groaned Titus, the eldest son of Tod Lazarus. "And, in the meantime, here's the Department of Transport wanting to run a bypass road across the hill, and Moko Supermarkets anxious to build a super store . . ."

Furiously he stamped on a beech-nut which a nervous squirrel had dropped from a branch overhead. Golden leaves were beginning to flutter down from the beeches.

The September sun shone warmly on the descendants of Sarah Lazarus as they paced about indignantly, reading copies of their grandmother's will.

"And what about this clause? Titania's Piece? Which field is that, anyway?"

"It's the strip of pasture-land beyond the beech trees," Mark Briskitt told his cousin Dinsie from Florida.

"What does Great-grandma mean when she says she is leaving it to the Travellers? Who are the Travellers, in mercy's name?"

"Travellers are gypsies. Egyptians, they

used to be called. I think they have always used this piece as a camp-ground, right back to the Middle Ages. I can remember when I was a boy," said Mark, "and I used to come here for holidays, quite often there would be half a dozen horse-drawn wagons up there. Once an old lady called Mrs Lee told my fortune." All of a sudden he looked wistful, remembering those days.

"She ever say you'd make a million?" big fat Saul Wodge asked with a guffaw.

"No . . . She said I'd come to the brink and step back from it. I often wondered what she meant . . ."

"But how could Great-grandma Lazarus leave Titania's Piece to the Travellers? Who *are* they? Do they have any legal rights?"

"Some of the local people round here say that piece of land always has belonged to them." Truda, the wife of Titus, a thin, dark girl, spoke hesitatingly.

"How could they ever prove that?" snapped Petunia Wodge.

"It's said there's a boggle-patch on that bit of land."

"And what," demanded Cousin Kent Lazarus from Poughkeepsie, "what, pray, is a boggle-patch?"

"It's an area of land surface that actually lies in another dimension. Belongs to other powers, you might say. So if you tread on it, for instance, you disappear," explained Mark, who was a professor of mathematics.

"Is that so?" demanded Saul Wodge, laughing even more heartily. "So, I just have to hike across that patch of pasture a few times, and I'll vanish clean away? Say! That would be a really *great* idea for a Fun Park. Let's give it a try!"

He strode off through the belt of trees to the rough downland turf beyond, and began methodically pacing backwards and forwards across it.

"Hey, Mark! How *big* is this alleged bogey-patch - or whatever you call it?" he shouted.

"Only about as big as a dinner-plate," Tansy, Mark's wife told him. She glanced about for her eight-year-old daughter. "Tish! Run and find your cousin Rickie and bring him down to the farmhouse for tea. It's time we were on our way."

Slowly all the cousins and second-cousins and their wives and children began to trickle away, leaving the high warm hill-side where fallen leaves lay on thin, fine grass.

Voices floated back in gusts on the after-noon breeze.

"Shame to break up the estate, really."

"A highway *and* a supermarket though - we'd all be millionaires . . ."

"But where can the Travellers be found? Do they have a legal address? Do they have a *lawyer*?"

"Who is Titania when she's at home?"

The sun slipped round the side of the hill. Dusk was beginning to creep into corners, under blackberry bushes, between the high straight trunks of beech trees.

Tish Briskitt and her cousin Rickie had found a hollow tree and made themselves a house in it.

Cousin Saul Wodge, red-faced and spluttering with laughter, still paced pertinaciously back and forth across the strip of grassland.

"Hey, watch me, fellas! I've just about covered it all, now!"

Nobody was paying much attention to him any more, except the two children, watching from their tree-house, and Cousin Mark from Manchester.

Tish's mother Tansy called the children again.

"Tish! Rickie! Will you come along now!"

But Rickie was wilful and made off, giggling and shrieking, in the opposite direction, after his grandfather Saul.

"Grandpa! Wait for me!"

"I'll catch Rickie!" shouted Tish. "I'll collar him, Mum! You'll see!"

Off she darted after Rickie, her black plaits flying out behind her.

Then they all saw big fat Saul suddenly vanish, like a match-flame blown out, like a thin sheet of glass turned sideways on.

"*Hey, fellas*!" he was calling, but his voice died away faintly on the wind.

Rickie, scudding after him, vanished in exactly the same way, two seconds later.

"*Mark*! NO!" shouted Mark's wife, rigid with horror, at the edge of the meadowland.

Mark, halfway across the grass in pursuit of his young cousin, pulled up and stood still.

So did his daughter Tish, just behind him.

"Dad!" she wailed. "Where's Rickie gone? Where is Uncle Saul?"

Husband, wife, daughter, looked at one another for a long, long minute, in complete silence. Then, still silent, taking hands, holding tight on to one another, they began to walk down to the farm, away from Titania's Piece.

The sun slipped behind the hill.

PETTICOAT PALM

When Joe went to stay with Grandma Quex the sea amazed him. For, where Joe lived, the sea was grey and flat, and it lay, dull and sad, on the other side of a grey flat stony beach.

But where Grandma Quex lived the sea was blue and clear, the colour of ink, and it roared and thrashed, in sheets of white foam, at the foot of a green grassy and black rocky cliff.

Grandma's palm tree stood on the top of the cliff and waved its fan-shaped branches wildly, as if it were sending messages to the tossing sea.

"Of course I have to take great care of it," said Grandma. "It is *much* too far north for a palm tree to be growing. But your grandfather planted it and I'd hate to lose it."

A date in her diary every six months was ringed with red ink and the letters DOT.

"That stands for Department of Trees," said Grandma. "They think my palm tree is so important that they send a man every six months to make sure I am looking after it properly."

Joe didn't see how you could look after a palm tree. But one morning the radio weather forecast said, "There will be severe ground frost tonight in northern counties, even in coastal areas. And the wind chill factor will make it even colder."

"My gracious," said Grandma Quex. "And it's this evening that the DOT man makes his call. You'll have to help me, Joe. We must wrap up the tree."

Grandma Quex had a big old stone house, which stood sheltered in a dent of the cliff. The top floor of the house was all huge attics, which held junk and treasures and mysteries from past times, going back hundreds of years.

"These things will do to wrap up the palm tree," said Grandma, opening trunks in one of the attics. And she pulled out petticoats and pantalettes and a huge quilted crinoline, as big as an air balloon. And she pulled out shawls and chemises and shirts, she pulled out vests and waistcoats and wigs and wrappers.

"Fetch out the kitchen steps, Joe," she said, "and we'll do this job properly."

Grishkin, Grandma's cat, sat watching them all through the afternoon as they wrapped and dressed the palm tree. He thought they had gone mad.

By the end of the afternoon there was not a single inch of the tree to be seen. They had wrapped up its furry, webby trunk in petticoats and crinolines. They had pinned shawls and wimples and yashmaks and cloaks and plaids and mantles over its fan-shaped branches.

Joe thought the tree looked terrific.

"If only it could dance," he said.

"Now the DOT man can come just as soon as he likes," said Grandma. "But I'm worn out. I'm going in to make a cup of tea."

The Evening Star came out while Joe was standing on the cliff, admiring Grandma's palm tree in its fancy dress.

"Star light, star bright," said Joe, "first star I see tonight, I wish I may, I wish I might, have the wish I wish tonight. I wish that palm tree could dance."

No sooner were the words out of Joe's mouth, then off danced the tree, tweaking itself out of the ground and capering down the steep hill as if it were happy to be set free at last!

"*Hey*!" bawled Joe. "Come back! You can't go off like that!"

But the tree paid no attention.

Where it had stood was a deep hole, with something flashing at the bottom. Joe reached down and grabbed whatever it was, then he set off at top speed after the palm tree. He was panting and gulping and horrified.

Somehow the palm tree had to be stopped, had to be brought back and set in

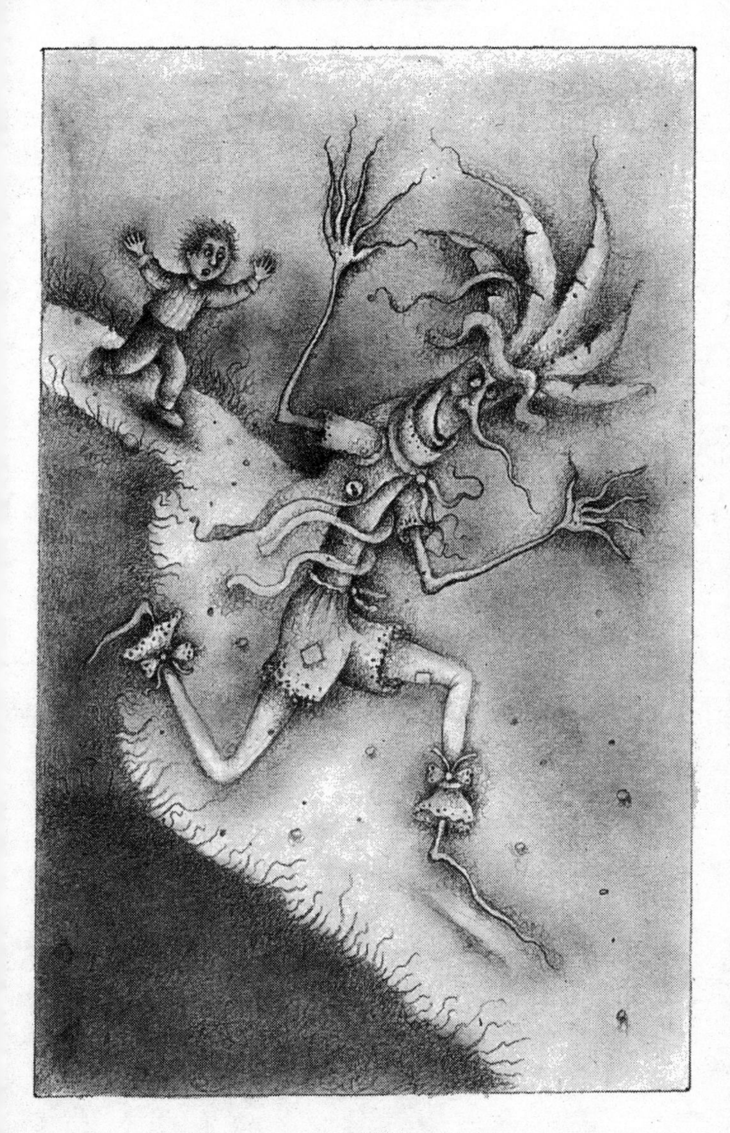

its place, before Grandma came out and saw what had happened, before the DOT man came on his visit of inspection. Or he might say that Grandma was not fit to be in charge of a palm tree.

The palm tree went dancing and skipping down the cliff path. It seemed quite drunk with joy. It bounced, it whirled, it leaned from side to side.

One thing, thought Joe, we tied those clothes on really tight, Grandma and I. At least they aren't coming off.

Joe had a piece of chalk in his pocket. He drew arrows on the path, in case Grandma came out, to show where they had gone.

Luckily at the foot of the cliff path there was a big puddle of water, where the waves had splashed over.

The palm tree stopped to admire its reflection, and Joe was able to catch up.

"Please, tree, go back where you belong!"

But the tree danced on down the path.

Now they came to a kissing-gate, a

wishing-gate, which was the entrance to the cliff path. The gate was like a stubby wooden cross, set on top of a post, and you pushed it round in order to go through. The palm tree edged its wrapped-up shape past the first arm of the kissing-gate.

And Joe cried out:

"Gate, gate, wishing-gate
Grant my wish, please don't wait
Please, please co-operate
Save my grandma from disgrace
Put the palm tree in its place!"

The palm tree cocked its branches to one side as if it listened. Then it spun through the kissing-gate - all the way round - and went dancing back up the path, as fast as it had danced down.

Joe went panting after, rubbing out the chalk arrows as he went.

And, when he got back to Grandma's house, he saw the palm tree jump into its hole and settle down with a shrug and a wriggle and a twitch.

Oh well! it seemed to be saying. I had a run. And I did have fun.

And it slipped in not a moment too soon, for there was the DOT man, coming up the road in his red car, and here was Grandma coming out of the old stone house.

"Well, sir!" she said proudly. "We've got our tree nicely wrapped up, as you can see!"

"You have indeed!" said the tree man. And he walked round the tree, admiring it.

Joe had a moment's horrible fright. Where was the cat, Grishkin? Could he possibly have been down in the hole, sniffing about, when the palm tree hopped back into place?

But then, with a huge gulp of relief, Joe saw Grishkin rubbing in a friendly way against the garden gate-post.

"No," said the tree man, walking round yet again. "The way you've got that tree snugged up, I reckon it should be good for another hundred years. And I'd not say no to a cup of tea, Mrs Quex!"

They went inside for a cup of tea. And Joe pulled out the shiny thing he had put in his pocket.

"Why!" said Grandma. "Where in the world did you pick that up? Your grandfather's watch, that's been lost since I was a young girl . . ?"

THE WORLD NEXT DOOR

Old Mrs Quill lived in a little black and white house by the side of a wood. Next to the house was an orchard, with twelve apple trees. In the spring the trees were covered with pink and white flowers. In the autumn they were hung all over with red and yellow fruit. Mrs Quill sold some of the apples, and gave many away to her friends, and ate the rest. And, as well, she made money by washing people's shirts and sheets and towels. She had clothes-lines hung between the apple trees, and every windy day there would be white and coloured laundry like flags blowing among the branches. The wind always blew on Mrs Quill's wash days.

The wind is my friend, said Mrs Quill.

Besides washing, Mrs Quill knew a great deal about how to cure pain. She often went into the wood, where she picked leaves and flowers and berries. From these she made pastes and pills and drinks which would send away almost any pain, headache, sore throat, stomach-ache or stiffness in the legs.

Mrs Quill gave her medicines to people; she never wanted money for her treatment.

"Everything in the wood is free," she said.

"How do you know so much, Mrs Quill?" a boy called Pip asked her.

"The wind tells me," she said. "I listen to the wind, in the leaves, in the branches. The wind comes from another world. My cottage stands by the wood. And the wood grows by a mountain. In the same way, this world floats by another world. And that is where the wind comes from."

Mrs Quill's old cat, Foss, purred and rubbed against her ankles.

"Foss knows about the wind," she said. "Foss goes into the wood at night, and hears it whispering secrets."

One day a big car stopped outside Mrs Quill's cottage, and a white-haired man got out. His name was Sir Groby Griddle.

"I am your new landlord, Mrs Quill," he said. "I have bought the wood, and the orchard, and the mountain. I plan to knock down your cottage and put a golf course on this land. You must find somewhere else to live."

"Leave my house?" said Mrs Quill. "But I was born in this house. I have always lived here. And so did my mother and grandmother."

"I can't help that," said Sir Groby. "The house has to come down. You will be found another one, somewhere else. Anywhere you like."

"But there would be no apple trees. And no wood where I could find plants. And nowhere to hang the washing."

They were standing under the apple trees as they talked. A white sheet blew out and flapped itself round Sir Groby. This annoyed him.

"All those apple trees must be cut

down," he said. "They are old and crooked. And the wood must come down as well. There will be a main road leading to the golf course. And a car park. And a clubhouse and a tearoom."

Mrs Quill said, "My cottage is very old. Hundreds and hundreds of years old. There is a law which says that old houses must not be pulled down."

The wind blew again, and a pillow-case flapped across Sir Groby's face. He was even more annoyed, because what Mrs Quill said was true. "You have not heard the last of this," he said.

He stamped away. A long roller towel blew out and flapped round his neck. He shouted, "You'll see, very soon! I always get my way in the end!"

After that, for many weeks, Mrs Quill was very quiet, thinking. She did not often smile. When people came to her house, asking for headache pills, or syrup for a sore throat, she was not always there.

"Where have you been, Mrs Quill?" the boy called Pip asked her one day, as she bandaged his grazed knee.

"In the wood. Tying threads round the trees."

"*All* the trees, Mrs Quill?"

"Yes. Every one."

"Why?"

"So that they will know me again. And I shall know them."

Now autumn had come. Mrs Quill's apples had all been picked. Lots of people helped her. The apples had been laid on shelves in her shed. They had a cool, sharp smell, which came floating out of the doorway, on the wind.

Once a year, Mrs Quill used to catch a bus and go into town to buy needles, and soap, and a new saucepan, and a garden fork. Things like that.

This year, on her way home, as she stood waiting by the bus-stop, she noticed a little black and white house on a patch of waste land near by.

That looks like my house, thought Mrs Quill.

But then a woman asked what would be

good for her little boy's ear-ache, and a man wanted a cure for chilblains. And then the bus arrived and Mrs Quill got on it, with her bundles.

But when she came to where her house had been, it was gone. The shed had been pulled down too. Apples were lying all over the ground, some of them squashed.

And there stood Sir Groby, smiling all over his face.

Men were in the orchard, sawing down the apple trees.

"I have had your house moved," Sir Groby told Mrs Quill. "I had it put on a truck, and moved to the edge of the town. That's quite legal. That's where you'll find it. It will be better for you there. You can go shopping, and see more people."

"Where is my cat Foss?" said Mrs Quill.

"He ran off into the wood," said a man who was halfway through sawing down a tree. "We'll find him tomorrow. We are going to cut down the whole wood."

Mrs Quill stood for a moment.

"Then I had better go into the wood

now," she said to Sir Groby. And she added, "You are going to miss that wood. You are going to need it. *And* the orchard, my orchard, that your men have cut down. You will be thirsty. All you can think about will be an apple. Your head will ache in the hot sun. All you need will be shade. But there will be no apple for you, and no shade."

A dry gust of wind blew from the wood and flung a handful of leaves against Sir Groby. They stung his eyes and scratched his cheeks. He shook his head angrily. When he could see again, Mrs Quill was walking away from him, into the wood.

"Let her go, silly old fool!" he said. "She'll come out soon enough, when we start cutting down the trees."

But Mrs Quill did not come out of the wood.

And when, next day, Sir Groby's men began cutting down the trees, a queer thing happened. As each tree was cut down, it shrank, like a slip of paper when you set a match to it, and vanished clean away. At the end of the day, instead of a huge pile of tree trunks, ready to be sold for timber, there was just nothing at all. Only some mud and a few leaves.

The roots were dug up and the land made flat and level. A golf course was laid out, and a car park. A red-brick clubhouse was built, with a flag on it.

But very few people came to play golf on the golf course. The ones who did told their friends that, at night, after playing, they had bad dreams. They dreamed they were trying to play golf in a forest. Trees and bushes grew up all round them. Leaves and prickles grew out of their golf clubs. Their balls rolled down rabbit holes. Nobody came back to play on Sir Groby's course a second time. He made no money from it.

The clubhouse stood empty. The flag dangled from its pole. No wind ever blew.

Sir Groby himself fell ill. His head ached all the time. Nothing would help the ache. All day long he was thirsty. He drank water, beer, milk, soda, wine, tea, coffee and champagne, but no drink would make the thirst go away.

And, every night, he dreamed about walking in a dark wood and listening to the wind.

At last he was so ill that he had to be taken to hospital.

"Where is Mrs Quill?" he kept asking. "And why does the wind never blow any more?"

"The wind *is* blowing, Sir Groby," the nurses told him. "A gale is blowing, outside the window, at this very minute. Can't you hear it roar?"

But he could hear nothing.

He lay ill for weeks and weeks. Nobody cared about him, so nobody came to see him, except a boy called Pip.

"I dream about Mrs Quill every night," Pip told Sir Groby. "In my dream I see her living in her cottage, with her wood, and her orchard. She is living in the world that floats next door to this one. You won't see her again."

"I don't want to hear about your dreams! All I want is something to cure this awful thirst," croaked Sir Groby.

"When I next see Mrs Quill in my dream I will ask her," said Pip.

Next day Pip came to the hospital again.

"In my dream I asked Mrs Quill about your thirst," he told Sir Groby. "She says that only an apple from her orchard will cure it."

"I don't believe you!" growled Sir Groby. "That's rubbish! In any case, her orchard is cut down, and there are no apples left."

A sudden gust of wind blew through the hospital room where Sir Groby lay. The window curtain sailed inwards and wrapped itself round Sir Groby's angry face. And a shower of dead leaves swept through the window like arrows and landed all over Sir Groby's bed.

"Good gracious!" cried a nurse, coming in. And she ran for a dustpan.

Sir Groby lay scowling, and said nothing at all for the rest of the day.

That night he dreamed that he was standing on the edge of the world, looking across the gap at the world that lay next door.

There was Mrs Quill's black and white

cottage, beside the orchard, beside the wood, beside the mountain. There was Mrs Quill herself, hanging out her washing, sheets and towels and pillow-cases, among the old twisted apple trees.

"I'm thirsty!" called Sir Groby, across the gap. "Oh, Mrs Quill, won't you help me? I'm so terribly thirsty!"

But Mrs Quill took no notice, just went on pegging out the towels and tea-cloths.

"Mrs Quill! I'm sorry I moved your house! I'm sorry I cut down your orchard! I"m sorry I cut down your wood! Won't you please tell me what will stop this awful thirst?"

At that Mrs Quill turned and looked at him. "Just being sorry is not enough," she said. "Hundreds of creatures had their homes in that wood - birds and mice, foxes, squirrels, rabbits, spiders, adders, bats, otters, hares and weasels. How can you put right the harm you did?"

"But I'm so thirsty!"

"Only an apple from my orchard will cure your thirst."

"But there aren't any left! They were all squashed and trampled."

"I have just one left here," she said. "See if you can catch it."

And she threw an apple across the gap.

But Sir Groby was not able to catch it. Down it fell - down and down - into the gap between the worlds, and was lost.

Mrs Quill turned and walked away into her orchard.

And Sir Groby, crying and wailing like a two-year-old, woke up from his dream. Next day he told the people at the hospital that he wanted to leave and go home.

"But you are not better," they said.

"I shall never be better if I stay here," said Sir Groby.

He sent for a car and a driver to come and fetch him.

On the way to Sir Groby's home, his car passed the bus-stop where Mrs Quill had caught her bus. But there was no black and white cottage on the site where Sir Groby's men had left it. Just a bare patch of ground with some bits of paper blowing about.

The boy, Pip, was standing and looking at the empty space.

Sir Groby opened his car window and called, "What happened to Mrs Quill's house?"

"It has gone," said Pip. "Just like the trees."

Sir Groby went home to his large, grand house. He ate roast beef for his supper, and drank champagne. But his head ached, just as badly as ever, and he was still thirsty.

At night, as he lay in bed, he heard the voices of all the creatures he had turned out of their homes, crying and grieving, squeaking and squawking, chirping and cheeping and chirruping.

He dreamed that he saw Mrs Quill, busy in the world next door, hanging out her wash. The wind was helping her.

"Mrs Quill! I will plant another wood, I promise!" he called to her across the gap. "Only, please, please, throw me one of your apples! I will plant another wood, and an orchard beside it."

At that she turned and looked at him more kindly.

"I do have just one more apple," she said. "See if you can catch it this time."

She tossed an apple across the gap. This time the wind gusted and blew the apple so that Sir Groby was just able to grab it. But just as he was about to take a big bite out of it, he woke up. Oh, what a blow that was, to wake and find he had no apple in his hand!

Sir Groby wailed like a two-year-old.

But then he struggled out of bed, and dragged on his clothes, and picked up his telephone, and gave orders for the golf club-house to be pulled down, and the car park dug up, and the golf course ploughed all over.

He ordered his car, and told the driver to take him to the golf course. On the way they passed by the bus-stop, where Mrs Quill's cottage had been left.

Sir Groby noticed that the empty waste patch was all covered with small green shoots, with young new leaves on them.

For it was spring now.

Sir Groby told his driver to stop, and got out of the car.

The boy Pip was standing and looking at the small trees.

"They are all seedling apple trees," he said.

A warm spring wind was blowing. It tossed the sprigs and leaves of the little seedling trees. The wind had a cool, sharp smell.

As it blew against his face, Sir Groby felt that the wind had come from a very long way off. Perhaps from another world. Perhaps from the world next door.

THE SILVER CUP

Jim's daily run for the newspaper took seven minutes. Two minutes up the sandy lane, one more to the paper-shop and back, three talking to Mr Stubbs, one running home downhill.

Mr Stubbs, an old sailor, swept the village street with a broom and a long-handled pan. "I like to be out every day talking to people," he said.

One morning Jim asked him about a pile of stones and sand in a plastic sack which had lain outside the post office for weeks.

"British Telecom folk left it," said Mr Stubbs. "I shan't touch it. Let 'em take it. Maybe if I shifted it, they'd turn me into a toad."

Another time, Jim asked about the two white-painted posts outside the *Green Dragon* pub, which had been knocked flat in the night.

"Maybe the Green Dragon did it," said Mr Stubbs.

A month before Christmas, Jim noticed a silvery metal cup wedged into the sandy bank at the corner where the lane met the village street.

"What do you think that is?" said Jim.

Mr Stubbs puffed out his white moustache thoughtfully. Today was very cold. Frost silvered the grass like sugar on strawberries. Mr Stubbs had on his blue knitted cap. His nose was as red as a strawberry.

"Tell you what," he said at last. "I think Santa Claus put that there for someone to make him a Christmas pudden."

"He did?" Jim was surprised. "Why?"

"He got no time to make his own, does he? Always driving round with those reindeer."

"But," said Jim, "Christmas only comes once a year."

"Ah? *Here*, that's so. But what about in space?" said Mr Stubbs. "What about out there? It's always Christmas somewhere, out there. Old Sandy Claws is at it the whole year long, dashing from one star to another. And the planets. And the sun. And all those moons. *He* don't get no three weeks' holiday."

"You think we ought to make him a Christmas pudding?" said Jim.

"I do," said Mr Stubbs.

"I'll ask Mum," said Jim.

Next day he told Mr Stubbs, "Mum says we can make a Christmas pudding if I can wash that cup really clean." He lifted the sandy metal cup out of the tuft of grass where it had lodged. "Mind you, Dad says it's only a hub-cap."

"Ah," said Mr Stubbs. "Off the sleigh, likely."

"Do sleighs have hub-caps?"

"Those that run on ball-bearings do." Mr Stubbs sniffed the frosty air. "Going to be a white Christmas. The birds think so, and they know."

"Why?"

"Cousins of Sandy Claws, they be. All that Claws family know about the weather. They know where it comes from. You can see 'em fly off the other way." He pointed. "See, the sky's all black in the north. And the birds is going south."

Jim took the silver cup home and rubbed and scrubbed and scraped it until his mum said it was clean enough to put Christmas pudding mix in.

She had been beating up eggs and milk and flour and butter and raisins and currants and candied peel and nutmeg and cinnamon and allspice and brandy; and, as well, she dropped in a thin, worn old silver penny piece, more than a hundred years old, which had belonged to Jim's great-granny. "For luck," she said. "Whoever finds it in his helping gets a wish."

"Even if Santa Claus finds it?"

"Of course."

When they had all stirred the gooey pudding mix it was spooned into three big bowls, and also the metal cup that Jim had brought home. Wax paper was laid on top, and cloths tied over, and the puddings were boiled for hours.

"When will they be done?" Jim kept saying, and Mum kept saying, "Not yet. Christmas pudding has to be cooked for a really long time."

The smell in the house while the puddings were cooking was so dark and rich and strong that you could have eaten the air with a spoon.

Outside, the birds had gone quiet. It was growing colder and colder. Every morning Jim scattered crumbs. Birds would come with a swish and flutter. Every crumb would be gone before Jim was back in the kitchen.

Smoke went straight up from the chimney, like a line ruled to the middle of the sky. The ground was hard as brick.

"Soon it'll snow," said Mr Stubbs.

But it didn't; not yet.

The puddings were put away at the back of the pantry, with the little one in its silver cup.

At last came Christmas Eve. Jim and his

dad walked to the woods and cut branches of holly and pine. They were stiff and rustly and smelt of magic. There was a sprig of mistletoe, with waxy white berries like pearls. And the Christmas tree was in a pot, ready to be hung with lights and shining balls. But that would not happen till Joe was in bed.

He hung up his stocking.

"Now can I leave Santa's pudding for him?" he asked.

"Wrap warm and run fast, then," said Mum. "For it's colder than I've ever known."

Dad went with Jim. It was dark. They could feel the frost crunch under their boots. The air was full of bell-music: tingle-tangle, dingle-dangle, ding-dong, dong, dong.

"You'd think the air would break in splinters," said Jim, sniffing its iciness.

The silver cupful of Christmas pudding was hidden carefully in the middle of a tuft of frosty grass.

"Will he be able to find it?" said Jim.

"Certain to," said Dad. "Let's run all the way home."

Next morning there was still no snow.

After undoing his stocking, and after breakfast, but before the presents on the tree were opened, Jim raced up the lane. There would be no newspaper, of course, on Christmas Day, but he wanted to see if Santa Claus had taken the pudding.

As Jim reached the village street, a few snowflakes began to fall. The sun, very low and red, had been trying to shine, but now it snuggled into a cloud, as if it had decided to go back to bed.

There was Mr Stubbs, with his broom.

"On Christmas?" said Jim, very surprised, but Mr Stubbs said, "People stay out late, Christmas Eve, and leave all kinds of rubbish. That's not nice for Christmas Day."

And he dropped two Coke cans and a crisp-bag into his pan.

Jim ran to the tussock where he and his dad had put the pudding, and found the cup was gone. There was a round dent where it had been.

He felt pleased, but also a little worried.

"It's gone," he said, "but how do we *know*

that Santa took it? Perhaps those people who dropped the Coke cans might have found it."

"Humph," said Mr Stubbs, tugging his moustache, staring at the sky. "That's true. "How *do* we know? That's a hard one."

But then he said, "Hey - boy! Look at the sky!"

Jim looked at the sky. The sun was still nestled behind a round, dark cloud. And out of the cloud, and other scattered clouds, flakes of snow, black and busy as bees, were pouring down.

And round the cloud, all the way round, like a flaming, many-coloured collar, there ran a rainbow. A complete circle of rainbow, bright and glowing.

"Well, blow me!" said Mr Stubbs. "A whole, round rainbow. I never in all my life at sea saw *that*!"

The snow pelted down, whitening the ground, and the rainbow hung, flashing, and the man and boy stood staring at it. Gradually it faded, as the snow fell thicker and thicker.

"Well," said Mr Stubbs, "reckon that was from old Sandy Claws to say thank you for his pudden. Now I'm off home, for I can't sweep up all this snow. And you'd best get back to your presents."

So Jim raced home down the lane, holding the rainbow inside his mind, like a silver cup.

THE KING OF THE FOREST

Yena was the daughter of the forester who lived in a hut on the edge of a great tree-covered stretch of land known as Marchwood. This name was given because the forest lay across the frontier between two dukedoms, and its ownership was always in dispute. Many wars had been fought about exactly where the boundary line would run; the bones of many forgotten soldiers lay buried under its overgrown rides and bridleways. Just now peace reigned in the region, but peace of a doubtful and uncertain kind. For, of the two dukes who now ruled over the lands on either side, one, Duke Vincent, was old and a trifle mad, while the other, Duke Gaylord, was young and impecunious, too poor to raise money and pay for an army.

There were some people, also, who held that the forest belonged to neither of the two dukes, but formed a separate region of its own, was really the property of some third and unknown prince, who would one day lay claim to the whole area, and put an end to these disputes.

Yena did not know, or care much, about these matters. Her life was very hard. She had plenty to do, cleaning the house, tending the vegetable patch, feeding the animals, avoiding her father's blows and her grandmother's harsh words. She knew only that her mother had died when she was born; she did not trouble her head as to the ownership of the forest. She herself was never allowed to stray very far among the trees; for one thing, there was always too much to do at home.

"Besides," said her grandmother, "the forest is full of ghosts, dragons, lawless men, werewolves and bears and hyenas. It's not a fit place for you to wander."

Once a year, only, Yena was allowed to go into the wood with her grandmother to put a bunch of primroses on her mother's grave. "To keep off evil spirits," said the old woman. Alone, Yena could never have found her way to the spot. The grave lay in a distant plot of ground. This land was a constant source of annoyance to Hugh, the forester. His master, Duke Vincent, had run a carriage-road across part of his meadow and, in compensation, had given him, not money but an equal-sized portion of ground far away in the forest. This little bit of grass-land, far distant among the trees, was no use to Hugh; he could not pasture sheep or pigs there, for they would be snatched by wolves; if he sowed corn on it, the seed was sure to be gobbled up by wild birds.

"You could try putting up a scarecrow?" Yena once suggested. The idea was prompted by a dream she had had.

Her father boxed her ears. "Fool girl! I tried that long ago. I put up two scarecrows. But the birds just jeered at them. In two days they were perching all over the arms."

"Go and feed the pigs, Yena," ordered her grandmother. "Girls should tend to their work and keep silent."

Yena's father had always, from the first, been furious that she was not a boy. "What use are girls?" he would growl, when he had drunk several mugs of sour cider, made from the half-wild apples off the trees in the garden hedge. "Why could I not have had a son, to learn the forester's trade?"

Twelve years after her mother had died, Yena's grandmother became ill, and crippled with rheumatism, and took to her bed. Yena took care of her faithfully, in spite of all the sour words she had from the old woman. She made milk porridge and black-currant tea, she rubbed the sick woman's joints with balsam, and her chilblains with goose grease.

"Well, you are not such a bad girl," grumbled the grandmother, now and then. "At least you are better than your mother ever would have been. She was a useless fine lady, if ever there was one! She had to put a clothes-peg on her nose before she fed the pigs, she could not stand the stink, she said. And she always had a bunch of dried violets in her buttonhole to sniff when she was cleaning out the privy."

"Oh, do please tell me more about my mother!" begged Yena, but only when her father was safely far out of the way.

At first the old woman would not. "It puts your father in a rage just to think of her. He believed she would bring him some great fortune. He believed she was the Duke's daughter. But what came of it all? Nothing at all, except a grave, out there among the trees. She's best forgotten. Just a useless fine lady who came walking out of the wood."

As the old woman grew weaker, she talked more.

"Well, *I* always thought that your mother came from the far side of the forest. Maybe after all she was Duke Gaylord's daughter, or his sister. But he lives at least a hundred miles to the west. How could she have walked as far as that?"

"Did my mother leave nothing at all? No token?"

"Nothing that your father didn't sell after she died. And those grass necklaces that she used to plait. Grass necklaces, indeed! I suppose you may as well have the last one. You will find it folded into my summer shawl."

Yena found the necklace, which was light as air, thin as a cobweb: a pale-green twist, cunningly plaited together from summer grass stalks when they are long and slender and shining and bear feathery seed-heads. Now I know something at least about my mother, thought the girl. I know how she felt and I know what she liked. I shall wear this always. "What was my mother's name?" she asked. But the grandmother was tired, and said, "I don't remember."

"She left nothing else?"

"A grass necklace and three babies."

Yena felt the blood turn backwards in her veins.

"Three babies, Grandmother? What *can* you mean? Three babies? Where are they?"

The old woman muttered an angry word at her own carelessness.

"I promised I'd not tell. Never let your father know that I spoke of it! He'd be in a rare rage with me."

"But, Grandmother, what do you mean? Three babies?" And Yena repeated, "Where are they?" She remembered the dream she once had, of two very small scarecrows, side by side, wearing babies' clothes.

Very carefully, she slipped a teaspoonful of blackcurrant jelly between her grandmother's lips.

The old woman swallowed, frowned, and said, "Well, I suppose it is all a long time ago now. Nobody could prove anything, I dare say. So I may as well tell you. This was the way it was. Your mother - a fine lady, and not used to the hard ways of the forest - she died, as you know, when you were born. And she left three babies behind her, three babies at a birth. All girls. Never, never shall I forget how angry your father was. It was in his mind to strangle the three of you, but I managed to stop him from doing that. 'Who is going to help *me*, in my old age?' I said. 'Since the mother is dead, leave me one to rear, to do the work of the house, to look after us later on.' And at last he saw the sense of that."

"What happened to the other two?" whispered Yena through chattering teeth.

"When he buried your mother, out there in the forest place, he left the other two out there as well, lying in their rush baskets under the stars."

"And?"

"And, who knows? He never went back - at least, not for six months. When he next went that way, it was winter. A foot of snow lay over the meadow. Who was to know what it hid? And when he went back a second time, in the spring, nothing was to be seen at all, except the grass and clover and cowslips and purple orchids."

"Not even the baskets?"

"Nothing. That's why he hardly ever goes near the place. Now, leave me in peace, girl. I'm tired out. I've talked more than I have strength for."

And indeed, when Yena next went to her grandmother's bedside, she found the old woman dead and stiff, her last piece of knitting clutched between her cold blue fingers.

In her turn, a grave was dug for her in the forest meadow.

"The bit of land is good for nothing else!" said Hugh angrily. "It becomes smaller every year, as seedling trees come sprouting up round the headlands. In five years it will be gone entirely."

The old lady's body, in its elm coffin, was lifted from the ox-cart and placed in the grave they had dug. Yena looked round, wondering where her sisters might lie. Then the father and daughter turned the ox, and went slowly back to the hut, which seemed even more silent now, lacking the old woman's peevish mumblings and pottering ways.

Hugh went about his regular work without speaking, often for days on end. He hardly ever looked at his daughter. If he did so, the sight of her only seemed to make him angry. For she was becoming beautiful, with a pale skin, red lips, long pale-gold hair, and dark eyes which were the greenish-grey of forest pools.

She, too, was very silent. As she performed her own tasks, feeding the geese, milking the cow, digging the potatoes, she kept thinking of her sisters. Once I had two sisters. Where are they now? What would they have been like? Perhaps one of them would have had a sweet singing voice and made up dozens of tunes, or songs. Perhaps the other would have been clever with words, put rhymes together, and stories, and riddles.

And, as Yena went about her work, she would hear, in her mind, the tunes that her elder sister might have sung, she would imagine, as she scrubbed the floor, as she peeled the potatoes, the stories and jokes and riddles that her younger sister might have invented.

"Why are you laughing?" her father sometimes growled.

"Oh - just something that came into my head!" And she would hand him a bowl of soup.

"Well, don't laugh!"

"What is that tune you keep humming?"

he would ask, another time.

"It just came into my mind."

"Well, keep quiet! Don't sing!"

So Yena tried to remember to wait until her father was away in the forest before she sang the tunes, or paid heed to the stories that sometimes floated into her mind.

When primrose time comes round again, she thought, I will leave a bunch of flowers on each of the graves - and two more for my sisters - then I will make my way through the forest to the other side. Maybe I shall find my fortune there.

What do I owe my father? Not a thing. I have worked for him all my life and had nothing in return but cuffs and curses.

Primrose time was long in coming that year. The winter lagged on into April. But now Yena could find her own way to the forest meadow where her mother and grandmother lay buried. After the grandmother's death she had followed the tracks of the ox-cart through the trees, and every day after that she went to lay bunches of autumn daisies or rose hips on the two graves. So now there was a clearly defined path to the place. Through snow and frost, Yena walked, and through mud and rain. As she went, she sometimes hummed to herself a rhyme that she had made up:

"Lost sisters, come to guide me
Ghost sisters, walk beside me."

Sometimes it almost seemed to her that she could hear the patter of soft footsteps beside her on the fallen leaves, or feel the touch of cool hands on either side, leading her along.

Now and then she met wild beasts, wolves or forest boar, once she met a pack of savage wild dogs, but she was not afraid of them.

She would whisper:

"Lost sisters, weave your charm
Keep me safe from hurt or harm."

And, whether because this made her bold enough to walk past the dangerous beasts without flinching, or because she herself was weaving a spell, the influence always worked, the wild creatures left her alone, and she was able to make her way peaceably through the forest.

But now a strange thing happened. When Yena went in April with her bunches of primroses to lay on the two graves, she found a man stretched out between them, dead.

He was a short, slender man, with delicate hands and feet. He is not so tall as my father, thought Yena; he is about my own size. He had strange long curly hair, snow-white, down to his shoulders, and his face, though unlined, was that of an old man.

A silver shell of armour covered his breast, and over that was a velvet surcoat with seven gold buttons the shape of acorns. He had a ring on his finger with a green stone in it the size of a chestnut. A silver sword lay beside him. A fur cloak wrapped him round.

"He must be some great lord!" breathed Yena. "I will have to tell my father."

Having placed her primrose bunches on the graves, she ran like the wind all the way back to the forester's cabin.

"Father, father! There's a grand prince lying dead in the forest field. I think he must be the King of the Wood!"

"What sort of man?" asked her father suspiciously. He found it hard to credit anything that Yena told him.

"Old, but not very tall. But so splendid! He has a silver sword and a big green stone in his ring, a gold chain, and a fur cloak. Do you think you should tell the Duke's bailiff? The poor man should have a proper funeral. Perhaps he is a king?"

"Not likely!" said her father. "But let's have a look at him. No call to go shouting to the bailiff. Come along, then, show me where he lies."

He slung a sack over his shoulder and set off after Yena into the forest.

When he saw the dead man, Hugh's eyes widened, and he said, "Well, to be sure! For once the wind of luck has blown my way. We'll trouble no bailiff with this fellow's affairs. I'll just bury him here, quietly, and that will be the end of him. *This* can come off, for a start."

And he twitched the gold ring off the dead man's finger.

"But, father!" said Yena, horrified. "You have no right to do that!"

Her father turned and dealt her a blow that made her stagger.

"Be quiet, you! Now, run home and bring the spade and the shovel. We'll dig his grave and cover him up so tidily that no one need ever know he was here. And if you so much as breathe a word to anybody about this, I'll thrash you till you can't stand."

Terrified, Yena ran home and fetched the spade and the shovel.

By the time she returned, her father had the man stripped bare, and all his things, the cloak, the armour, the velvet vest, the ring, the chain, the sword, were stowed away in the sack.

"Now help me dig his grave," ordered Hugh.

This took several hours, for the forest earth was hard and rocky.

As they did it, Yena grew more and more afraid. Not of wild beasts; nor that the Duke's men might come and see what they were doing; she was afraid of she knew not what.

The day was dwindling to its close; dark would soon come.

"Good," said the forester at last. "That should be deep enough. Now, help me lift the fellow in. It's good he's so slight and puny. You take his feet, I'll take his shoulders."

Yena did not like holding the dead man's feet. They felt icy cold. But she obeyed her father.

Just as the body was laid in the bottom of

the grave, they heard a blood-freezing growl, a howl, from among the young trees that grew thickly round the sides of the little meadow. And a great grey shape came pushing its way out from the saplings.

"Save us!" said Hugh. "It's the great grey bear from Wanbrook Dell. *Run*, girl! He'd eat you in two bites. You go one way, I'll go another, he won't know which to chase - *run*!"

Snatching up the sack, Hugh took to his heels.

The huge beast paused, hesitating, turning his head from side to side.

Yena stood still.

"Ghost sisters, make me brave
Help me now, keep me safe!"

she whispered.

The great beast shook itself all over. Then it stomped slowly across the grass and peered into the open grave. Then it let out a great moaning bellow, like the sound of two forest boughs rubbing together in a gale. Then it lumbered swiftly away, following the direction that Hugh had taken.

Yena thought: I can't help my father. I must cover the dead man decently. That, at least, I can do for him.

She took off the grass chain that her mother had plaited, that her grandmother had given her. I can't give the dead man back his ring and his sword, she thought; but at least I can give him this to carry into the next world, to show that people thought well of him in this one.

She slipped the grass necklace over her head and knelt by the grave to loop it over the dead man's head.

But now, no dead man lay there! Only a huge beam of wood, grey and ridged with age. It looked as if it might have lain in that spot for fifty years.

Trembling, Yena scraped all the loose earth back into the grave, and trod it down.

Then she stood up, wondering whether to go back to the hut, or to start now, directly, on her perilous journey through the forest to the other side. Dark had fallen. How would she ever find her way? And to what place?

"Lost sisters, come to guide me
Ghost sisters, walk beside me,"
she called.

Yena felt two soft cold hands, slender fingers that seemed to be made of mist, gently catch hold of hers and lead her forward towards the heart of the forest.

Duke Vincent's bailiff, coming to the forester's hut next day, found it empty and cold. The fire was out, the animals clamouring to be fed. Half a mile away, Hugh the forester was found lying on a path where a branch of a huge oak tree had fallen on him and crushed him to death. Underneath him was a sack of dead leaves.

The forester's daughter was never seen again.

WHEELBARROW CASTLE

Colum was up in his Aunt Eily's room when, through the window-hole, he saw the Viking ships. Three galleys with sharp evil prows like the beaks of hawks were slicing their way briskly southward over the dark-blue sea.

The boy felt a cold grip of fear on his ribs.

As, indeed, he might. Viking raiders had killed his father and mother, long ago, when he was too young to remember. But Aunt Eily had told him the story, many times, of how she had hidden with him in a sea cave until the invaders had been and gone, leaving ruin and sorrow behind them. During three tides, the girl and the small child had waited, hidden in the cave, until the shouts and screams, and the smell of burning, had died away.

But that was many years back. Vines and vegetables had grown again, cattle and poultry had been brought from other islands. For a long peaceful stretch of years the Vikings had not come raiding. Colum had grown into a tall, strong boy in the course of that time. And now, just last week, Aunt Eily had died from the sting of a blue, poisonous fish. Perhaps it was she, her magic power, which had been keeping the Vikings away all this time? For Aunt Eily was a witch. In her little blue-walled chamber, high up under the castle roof, she pounded herbs and murmured runes. She could heal wounds, mend broken bones, and cure many illnesses. But not her own, it seemed.

"Take care of my magic things, Colum, boy," she gasped, as she lay dying on the shore. "It is most likely the power will come to you now. Use it well! Look after the folk. See well, watch well - hear well, listen well . . . " And then she laced her long thin fingers across her eyes, calling in a faint voice, “My sister, my brother, wait for me! I am coming!”

After his Aunt Eily had been buried, among the vines on the sunny hillside, Colum went up to her little dark-blue room.

All the people of the island lived in what was called the High City, or the Wheelbarrow Castle, which was a huge old castle left behind on the top of the hill by the Romans, long, long, long ago. The walls of it were so massive-strong that Colum’s grandparents, and his great-great-grand-parents, and *their* parents, had burrowed out an entire town in the thickness of them; whole houses and streets had been bored through the mighty ancient Roman fortifications; folk lived there snug and sociable together as bees in a hollow tree. And Aunt Eily, high under the ramparts in her little blue kitchen, had been for many years their wise-woman and watch-woman.

“And you will be so after me, Colum my boy,” she sometimes said to her nephew.

But Colum had always answered obstinately that he would prefer to be a poet.

When he reached the age of ten years, Colum made himself a wheelbarrow, carved the strong white wheel from a log of driftwood, wove the body from willow withes, and cut the handles from the mast of a shipwrecked galley broken up on the shore by furious north winds.

From the use of this barrow he was able to make a living. "I will carry any weight for anybody to any place!" was his cry, and the people of the island were ready enough to employ his strength when shifting their pigs, or their sacks of grain, or loads of rocks for building, or fish from the shore. And while Colum hoisted heavy weights and trundled them all over the island, he was busy in his mind making up rhymes and setting them to music.

"Wild waves, wild waves, growing so high
Waves in the sea, and fish in the sky
Ninth wave, ninth wave, stay far from me
Laugh with your brothers in the halls of the sea
Roar with your brothers in the halls of the sea . . ."

Colum would sing to himself as he transported the miller's flour, or the headman's nets, or a neighbour's pig, or the keel of a boat.

"A wave-way here, a wave-way there,
A wind-way here, cutting through the air
Soft sand leaves no footprint
Bright flame leaves no trace
Only man looks in the glass
And sees his own face."

Aunt Eily, listening to Colum's songs at the evening time, over the smoke of the supper-fire, would say, "Ay, ay, it's true, songs must be sung, but there's more than songs needed when trouble comes southward over the sea." Now trouble *was* coming southward, and Colum did not know how to meet it.

Below him he could hear the castle stirring like a colony of ants when the spade breaks through the dome of their nest. He could hear mothers wailing and babies crying and the shouts of men, gathering their weapons together. But there were only twenty men, just at present, in Wheelbarrow Castle, and these were the old ones, or the lame and afflicted; all the rest were gone away on the fishing tides and could not be back for some days.

What would they return to?

It is up to me to stop this trouble somehow, Colum thought. But what can I do? Aunt Eily, help me now!

His eyes wandered round her little dark-blue room, past the wooden bowls and the dried leaves, the pages of magical books, the glass eye from a mermaid's treasure chest, the shawl made from seal's fur, and the hearing-stone. His eye paused on the hearing-stone, which Eily had found washed up on the shore, one dark winter day. It fitted in her ear exactly.

And now Colum fitted it into his own ear. And the stone began to whisper.

"Criss-cross, criss-cross row
When I look through the criss-cross row
Grow, *grow*!
Fingers short, fingers tall
Window-bars for a soul's hall
When I peer through fingers tall
Grow small!"

Hearing this voice Colum began to remember a game that Aunt Eily must have played with him many times when he was a tiny lad, wandering on the shore by the rock pools.

She would press her hands against her face, peering at him through the slits between the fingers. And then she would sing her rhyme: "Grow small! Grow small!"

And he - yes, he truly had - he had grown small at her command, smaller than a mouse, small as a bee or a sand-hopper, so that the flowers of thrift, growing by the beach, seemed to him like huge scented cushions, so that the seaweed was like a mighty tangle of rope, so that the rock-pools were huge lagoons and the grains of sand were boulders.

This had really happened, many times. He could remember it. And he had found jewels for Aunt Eily, treasures, and tiny magic plants. Then, when it was time to go home for supper, she would criss-cross her fingers over her face, making a lattice, and call out:

Wheelbarrow Castle

"When I look through the criss-cross row
Grow, grow!"

and so restore Colum to his true size.

But could *I* do that? wondered Colum. Would it happen for me, as it did for Aunt Eily?

He raced down the stairs, steep winding stairs that had been chewed out of the thickness of the wall. In the street outside Aunt Eily's door people were running and crying, bumping into each other in their hurry and terror; women clutched hens and slapped at pigs which had been fetched in from the hillside; aged trembling men sharpened rusty spears and fitted strings to their bows.

Colum grabbed up the handles of his wheelbarrow, which had stood at the foot of the stair, and pushing it, made his way towards the castle entrance.

"Where are you off to, boy?" shouted the head-man, who had not gone with the fishing party, for he had an arm broken in a gale.

"To get rocks - rocks to throw from the walls," panted Colum.

"Rocks! Rocks will be little use against those northern devils," growled the head-man, but Colum had already dodged away among the panicking people, and was out of the castle gate and scampering down the steep hillside path, which led from the entrance to the harbour in a series of sharp zig-zag bends. Nobody remained on the path now but himself; all the rest had gathered their goods - what they could carry - and retreated inside the castle gate.

A shout came down for him.

"Colum! Come back! We are going to bar the gate! Come back inside!"

Colum stopped at the fourth bend to catch his breath. He looked downhill and saw that the three Viking ships had swept into the harbour. Men were spilling out of them - at least thirty men from each boat. They wore iron caps and carried thick massive swords that gleamed in the pale spring sun. A wild exultant shout came from them as they hurled themselves ashore.

Colum turned and looked at the castle above him. He pressed his fingers across his face, stared at the castle through the slits between the fingers, and whispered,

"Fingers short, fingers tall
Window-bars for my soul's hall
Grow small!"

And - at once - to his almost disbelieving, amazed joy, the castle began to shrink and shrink, with all its terrified inmates inside it - shrank until it was the size of a seal, a sheep, a salmon. When it was small enough to carry, Colum ran back up the hill, plucked the castle from the ground like a loose boulder, and dropped it into his wheelbarrow. Then he raced with it down the far side of the hill - ran, and ran, with his heart bursting in his chest, until he reached the shore. He dared not wait to see what the Vikings were doing behind him, although he would dearly have liked to find out how they behaved when they discovered that the goal they had come all this way to plunder was gone, vanished, leaving only a bare hill-top. But there was no time for looking back. He was responsible for the castle and all those living beings inside it. Colum ran

Wheelbarrow Castle

along the shore until he came to the cave where Aunt Eily had once hidden him. He guided his wheelbarrow inside it - far, far in, for he had been back into the cave many times, and knew its windings as well as he knew the passages of the castle itself.

Then he waited. The tide was rising, but Colum hoped that he had brought the castle, and its dwellers, high above the level of any but the highest spring-tides.

Will that be high enough, though? he wondered. Here the cave roof came lower, he could push the castle no farther. All he could do was wait and hope.

"Ninth wave, ninth wave, stay away from me
Laugh with your brothers in the halls of the sea."

For three high tides Colum waited; then at last he ventured out.

Vikings, he knew, never stayed long, even in a place they had plundered. And what would there be to wait for here, with the castle gone?

When he ventured out on to the shore

again, pushing the laden wheelbarrow - and a heavy, frightening weight it now seemed to him, with no knowledge of how the inhabitants had fared during that time in the cave, and no certainty now that he could restore them again to their true size - Colum found a terrible storm raging over the island. The waves hissed like snakes, the winds howled like dragons. Ribbons of snow cut his face as he slowly pushed the wheelbarrow back up the hill path. Sore was the weight on his arms, and sore the weight on his heart. For what of the fishers who had gone off, many days ago now, where were they?

When he reached the hilltop Colum stooped, panting, and braced himself, and hoisted the castle, with all its load of inhabitants, living or dead - hoisted it out from the barrow and settled it back into the empty slot on the hillside where it had stood before. Then, staggering slightly, on legs that felt like skeins of sheep's wool, he made his way back to the fourth bend of the road, latticed his fingers across his eyes, and called out loudly:

"When I look through the criss-cross row
Grow - *grow* - *GROW*!"

And, to his infinite thankfulness and joy, he saw the castle, through the dark and flying snow, begin to stretch itself and rise, like a loaf in the oven - rise, rise and rise, until it towered above him.

At this sight, Colum's strength gave out entirely, and he fell face-down among the heather at the side of the pathway, and so lay, as if he were stunned, until daybreak roused him.

At which time he looked up, and saw folk coming out of the castle, going about their normal day's business, driving out the pigs and poultry, grieving over the vines and pot-herbs and kitchen plants that the Vikings had spoiled - but, at least, all alive - alive, not shrivelled, not shrunk, not drowned, not slaughtered, just the familiar folk going about their usual business.

And, looking *down* the hill, Colum saw the harbour tossing with wreckage, and he recognised the curved prows of the Viking ships. And, looking out to sea, he saw the fishing boats coming back over the dark-blue water . . .

When the fishermen rejoined their families in the castle there was great joy, and great perplexity. For the harbour was full of the shattered remnants of the Viking ships, and dead bodies of drowned Viking warriors who had been dashed against the harbour walls for two days by wild northerly gales, and unable to put out to sea.

"But why did the Vikings not come up the hill - attack the castle?" was asked, over and over. Nobody knew the answer to that question. All that the wives and mothers, all that the old men and the invalids could tell was that, for the duration of three tides, a great darkness had fallen over the castle, and a great silence had reigned. It was like the Day of Judgment. It was like being in a cave. Nobody had left or entered the castle. No Vikings had been seen or heard.

"But the Vikings must have been just outside the castle, for they smashed the vines and trampled the young corn," said one of the mothers.

No Vikings were left alive to tell what they had found. All had been drowned as they tried to put out to sea against the furious northerly winds.

And Colum, meanwhile, kept his own counsel, as he pushed his wheelbarrow and made up his rhymes.

"Soft sand leaves no footprint
Bright flame leaves no trace
Only man looks in the glass
And sees his own face . . ."

If you enjoyed these stories,
look out for Joan Aiken's

Fog Hounds
Wind Cat
Sea Mice

Also available from
Hodder Children's Books.

Turn the page for a taster . . .

A BOY CALLED TAD WAS painting the front door of the house where he and his sister lived, one mild September evening. Using fast-drying paint, he was painting the door a beautiful honeysuckle yellow, and he had nearly finished the job, which was just as well, for dusk was beginning to wrap the village in shadows. Very few people were about, and lights were twinkling out, one by one, in the cottage windows.

The boy's sister, Ermina, rattled the curtains apart and put her head out of the front window.

'Tad? Haven't you finished yet?' she called. 'Make haste, it's nearly Hound Time.'

In the country where Tad and Ermina lived, it was dangerous to be out of doors after sunset. The reason for this was the tribe of huge misty creatures, known as the Fog Hounds, which roamed all over the land from dusk to dawn; they went ranging and loping through towns and villages, past factories and farms, through fields and forests. Their feet made no noise on the ground, they were pale grey and half transparent, like smoke, so that you could see lamp-posts and letter-boxes through them and beyond them. Most of the time they ran along silently, with their noses down close to the ground, but every now and then one of them would lift his head and howl, and when he did, what a blood-curdling sound *that* was! It almost made the blood run backwards in your veins.

Nobody who had been chased by the Fog Hounds ever came back alive to tell the tale of what had happened to him. The hounds belonged to the King, and were supposed to chase only criminals and wrongdoers. But the King was old, very old and sick, and had lost most of his wits; it was said that he didn't care what the hounds did any more.

So Ermina called anxiously: 'Tad! Come along! Leave the door if you haven't finished, it must wait till the morning. Come inside!'

Ermina was fifteen years older than her brother; and she was a Wise Woman, which is halfway to being a witch. She possessed a pack of cards which could fly, like a flight of swallows, from one of her hands to the other; and she could read people's futures in tea-leaves or apple-peelings or duck-feathers.

She made a living by advising people,

and telling them what to do if they were unable to make up their minds. The only future she could not read was that of Tad, her own younger brother. When she looked at the cards or the tea-leaves they told her nothing about him; and that was why she worried whenever she thought he might be taking a risk.

'It's all right, Minnie,' Tad called back now. 'I'm just putting on the last lick of paint.'

He did so, admired his work, and was about to open the door and step inside the house, when he heard hasty, running footsteps, and a voice that called frantically, 'Stop, stop! Wait! Help me, please help me!'

Tad waited, with the paint-pot in one hand, and the brush in the other, and he saw a man running at full speed along the village street. A very queer-looking man he was – Tad had never seen anything like him before. On one side of his head the hair was black; on the other side it was white. One of his eyes was blue, the other was brown. One of his hands was black, the other was white; and his jacket and trousers were divided down the middle, red on the left, black on the right.

He was dusty and muddy and his clothes were ragged, and he ran with a stumble and a limp. Sweat poured down his cheeks and he seemed ready to fall to the ground from weariness yet he was running at a desperate speed and kept looking back over his shoulder in terror. 'They're after me!' he panted.

'Who are?' said Tad, though he guessed.

'The King's soldiers. The Fog Hounds. Save me, oh, save me!'

Then Tad noticed that in the man's left hand - which was the black one - he clutched a golden sprig - it had a flower and leaves and roots; it seemed to be alive, yet it seemed to be made of pure gold.

At this moment, in the distance Tad thought he could hear a sound of sirens wailing, horns blowing, hounds giving tongue, and the clatter of hoofs.

The front window flew open again and Ermina put her head out a second time.

'*Tad!* Make haste and come inside!'

Then she saw the stranger on the footway and said sharply, 'Why are you keeping my brother out of the house? Don't you know it is dangerous? It is almost Hound Time. Who are you?'

'My name is Doubleman,' said the stranger. 'The King's soldiers are after me. I beseech you to save me!'

'Why are they after you? What did you do wrong? Why should we save you? If we take you in, we shall be in danger too,' argued Ermina.

Now the sound of galloping hoofs and wailing sirens could be heard much closer; and also the dreadful throaty pealing bay of the Fog Hounds.

'I helped myself to a golden sprig from the Royal Mint,' said the stranger. 'The hounds have scented it; that is why they are after me.'

'Throw it away, then,' said Ermina. 'What right had you to take it?'

'Throw it away?' panted the man. 'After I had gone to so much trouble to steal it? Never!'

His breath streamed out of his mouth in a white cloud, like the smoke from acid. Tad noticed that a rose growing by their gate began to wither, where the stranger had breathed on its leaves and flowers; they turned black, and shrank together, and fell from their stalks.

The man coughed several times and drew in deep, hacking breaths. Then he pulled a cigarette from his pocket, blew on the tip until it glowed scarlet, put it into his mouth, and sucked heavily on it.

'Tad! Come inside!' Ermina cried shrilly. 'It's mad to stay out there. We can't help you at all,' she told the stranger. 'If you robbed the Royal Mint, then you must look out for yourself.'

'Could you keep the golden sprig for me? If it's not on me, perhaps the hounds won't catch me–'

'And have them catch us instead? Not likely!' said Ermina, and she flung open the front door, dragged Tad inside, and then slammed the door and bolted it.

The stranger called Doubleman glanced hastily up and down the street, dragging hard on his cigarette as he did so, until the tip glowed gold. Then he ran on a few yards, and tossed the golden sprig into a builders' rubbish skip which stood a short way along the road, outside an empty house. Leaving the sprig there, Doubleman ran on, going faster and more easily after his short rest; soon he had vanished into the dusk.